Catherine Crowe

Ghosts and Family Legends

e-artnow 2020

Catherine Crowe

Ghosts and Family Legends

Horror Stories & Supernatural Tales

e-artnow, 2020
Contact: info@e-artnow.org

ISBN 978-80-273-0575-9

Contents

Preface

It happened that I spent the last winter in a large country mansion, in the north of England, where we had a succession of visitors, and all manner of amusements-dancing, music, cards, billiards, and other games.

Towards the end of December, 1857, however, the gaiety of the house was temporarily interrupted by a serious misfortune that occurred to one of the party, which, in the evening, occasioned us to assemble with grave faces round the drawing-room fire, where we fell to discussing the slight tenure by which we hold whatever blessings we enjoy, and the sad uncertainty of human life, as it affects us in its most mournful aspect-the lives of those we love.

From this theme, the conversation branched out into various speculations regarding the great mysteries of the here and hereafter; the reunion of friends, and the possible interests of them that have past away in the well-being of those they have left behind; till it fell, naturally, into the relation of certain experiences which almost everybody has had, more or less; and which were adduced to fortify the arguments of those who regard the future as less disjoined from the present than it is considered to be by Theologians generally.

In short, we began to tell ghost stories; and although some of the party professed an utter disbelief in apparitions, they proved to be as fertile as the believers in their contributions-relating something that had happened to themselves or their friends, as having undoubtedly occurred, or to all appearance, occurred-only, with the reservation, that it must certainly have been a dream.

The substance of these conversations fills the following pages, and I have told the stories as nearly as possible in the words of the original narrators. Of course, I am not permitted to give their names; nobody chooses to confess, in print, that he or anybody belonging to him, has seen a ghost, or believes that he has seen one. There is a sort of odium attached to the imputation, that scarcely anyone seems equal to encounter; and no wonder, when *wise* people listen to the avowal with such strange incredulity, and pronounce you at the best a superstitious fool, or a patient afflicted with spectral illusions.

Under these circumstances, whether I have ever seen a ghost, myself, I must decline confiding to the public; but I take almost as courageous a step in avowing my entire and continued belief in the fact that others do occasionally see these things; and I assert, that most of those who related the events contained in the ensuing pages of this work, confessed to me their absolute conviction that they or their friends had actually seen and heard what they said they did.

Some of the company related curious traditions and legends connected with their family annals; and these form the second part of this little book, which I hope may prove a not uninteresting companion for a Christmas fireside.

CATHERINE CROWE.

15th *October*, 1858.

First Part
Round the Fire

"But there are no ghosts now," objected Mr. R.

"Quite the contrary," said I; "I have no doubt there is nobody in this circle who has not either had some experience of the sort in his own person, or been made a confidant of such experiences by friends whose word on any other subject he would feel it impossible to doubt."

After some discussion on the existence of ghosts and cognate subjects, it was agreed that each should relate a story, restricting himself to circumstances that had either happened to himself or had been told him by somebody fully entitled to confidence, who had undergone the experience.

We followed the order in which we were sitting, and Miss P. began as follows: —

"I was some years ago engaged to be married to an officer in the —— regiment. Circumstances connected with our families prevented the union taking place as early as we had expected; and in the mean while Captain S., whose regiment was in the West Indies, was ordered to join. I need not say that this separation distressed us a good deal, but we consoled each other as well as we could by maintaining a constant correspondence; though there were no steam packets in those days, and letters were much longer on their way and less certain in their arrival than they are now. Still I heard pretty regularly, and had no reason for the least uneasiness.

"One day that I had been out shopping, and had returned rather tired, I told my mother that I should go and lie down for an hour, for we were going out in the evening, and I was afraid I might have a head-ache, to which I am rather subject; so I went up to my room, took down a book and threw myself on the bed to read or sleep as it might happen. I had read a page or two, and feeling drowsy had laid down the volume in order to compose myself to sleep, when I was aroused by a knock at my chamber door.

"'Come in,' I said, without turning my head, for I thought it was the maid come to fetch the dress I was going to wear in the evening.

"I heard the door open and a person enter, but the foot was not her's; and then I looked round and saw that it was Captain S. What came over me then I can't tell you. I knew little of mesmerism at that period, but I have since thought that when a spirit appears, it must have some power of mesmerising the spectator; for I have heard other people who had been in similar situations describe very much what I experienced myself. I was perfectly calm, not in the least frightened or surprised, but transfixed. Of course, had I remained in my normal state, I should either have been amazed at seeing Captain S. so unexpectedly, especially in my chamber; or if I believed it an apparition, I should have been dreadfully distressed and alarmed; but I was neither; and I can't say whether I thought it himself or his ghost. I was passive, and my mind accepted the phenomenon without question of how such at thing could be.

"Captain S. approached the bedside, and spoke to me exactly as he was in the habit of doing, and I answered him in the same manner. After the first greeting, he crossed the room to fetch a chair that stood by the dressing table. He wore his uniform, and when his back was turned, I remember distinctly seeing the seams of his coat behind. He brought the chair, and having seated himself by the bed side, he conversed with me for about half-an-hour; he then rose and looking at his watch, said his time had expired and he must go; he bade me good bye and went out by the same door he had entered at.

"The moment it closed on him, I knew what had happened; if my hypothesis be correct, his power over me ceased when he disappeared and I returned to my normal state. I screamed, and seized the bell rope which I rang with such violence that I broke it. My mother, who was in the room underneath, rushed up stairs, followed by the servants. They found me on the floor in a fainting state, and for some time I was unable to communicate the cause of my agitation. At length, being somewhat calmed, I desired the servants might leave the room, and then I told my mother what had happened. Of course, she thought it was a dream; in vain I assured her it was not, and pointed to the chair which, wonderful to say, had been actually brought to the bedside by the spirit-there it stood exactly as it had been placed by him; luckily nobody had moved it. I said, you know where that chair usually stands; when you were up here a little while ago it was in its usual place-so it was when I lay down —I never moved it; it was placed there by Captain S.

"My mother was greatly perplexed; she found me so confident and clear; yet, the thing appeared to her impossible.

"From that time, I only thought of Captain S. as one departed from this life; suspense and its agonies were spared me. I was certain. Accordingly, about a month afterwards, when one morning Major B. of the —- regiment sent in his card, I said to my mother, 'Now you'll see; he comes to tell me of Henry's death.'

"It was so. Captain S. had died of fever on the day he paid me that mysterious visit."

We asked Miss P. if any similar circumstance had ever occurred to her before or since.

"Never," she answered; "I never saw anything of the sort but on that occasion."

"I have no experience of my own to relate," said Dr. W., "but in the course of my late tour in Scotland, I went amongst other places to Skye, and I found the whole island talking of an event that had just happened there, which may perhaps interest you. There was a tradesman in Portree of the name of Robertson; I believe he was a sort of general dealer, as shopkeepers frequently are in those remote localities. Whatever his business was, however, it frequently took him to the other islands or the mainland to make purchases. He had arranged to go on one of these expeditious, I think to Raasa, when a friend called to inform him that a meeting of the inhabitants was to be held on some public question in which he, Robertson, was much interested."

"'You had better defer going till after Friday,' said Mr. Brown; 'we can't do without you, and its very possible you may not get back in time.'

"'Oh, yes, I can do all my business, and be back very well on Thursday,' said Mr. Robertson; objecting that if he waited over Friday it would be no use going till Monday. Brown tried to persuade him to alter his plans, but in vain; 'however,' said he, 'you may rely on seeing me on Thursday, if you'll look in, in the evening; as I would not miss the meeting on any account.'

"This conversation took place at an early hour on Tuesday morning. Immediately afterwards Mr. Robertson bade his wife and children good-bye, and proceeded to the boat which left at eleven o'clock, having on board, besides himself, two other passengers, and two boatmen.

"On Thursday evening, Mr. Brown, who had been busying himself in fortifying and encouraging their adherents against the next day, and had taken upon himself to answer for his friend Robertson's presence, as soon as he had finished business, set off to keep his appointment with the latter, anxious to ascertain that he was arrived.

"His anxiety was soon relieved, for on his way he met him.

"'Well, here you are,' said he, holding out his hand.

"'Yes,' answered Robertson, not appearing to notice the hand, 'I have kept my promise.'

"Upon that Mr. Brown introduced the subject of the meeting, and mentioned the hopes he had of carrying the question, with which Robertson seemed satisfied; but as soon as possible turning the conversation into another direction, he began talking to his friend about his wife and children, and certain arrangements he had wished to be made respecting his property.

"His mind seemed so much more engrossed with these matters than the meeting, that little was said upon the latter subject, and Mr. Brown, having parted with him in the street, rather wondered why he chose such a moment to discuss his private affairs.

"The next morning, at the appointed hour, the principal inhabitants of the place assembled in a public room at the Tun. Brown, who wanted to say a word to Robertson, lingered at the door; but as he did not come, he thought he must have arrived before himself, and went up stairs.

"'Is Robertson here?' said he, on entering the room.

"'No,' said one, 'I'm afraid he's not come back from Raasa.'

"'Oh, yes,' said Brown, 'he'll be here; I saw him yesterday evening.'

"They then discoursed about the matter in hand for some time, till finding the chairman was about to proceed to business, Robertson's absence was again reverted to.

"'I know he's come back,' said one, 'for I saw him standing at his own door as I passed last night.'

"'He can't have forgotten it,' said another.

"'Certainly not, for we spoke of it last night,' said Brown.

"'Perhaps he's ill,' suggested somebody.

"'Just send your man to Mr. Robertson's, and say we are waiting for him,' said Brown to the landlord.

"The landlord left the room to do so; and, in the meantime, they proceeded to business.

"Presently, the landlord re-entered the room, saying, that Mrs. Robertson answered that her husband had not returned from Raasa, and that she did not much expect he would be back till night.

"'Nonsense,' cried Brown, 'Why, I saw the man yesterday according to appointment, and had a long conversation with him.'

"'I am sure he's come back,' said one who had spoke before. 'I was coming down the street on the other side of the way, and I saw him standing at the door with his apron on. I should have crossed over to speak to him, but I was in a hurry.'

"'It's extraordinary,' said the landlord: 'Mrs. Robertson declares he's not come.'

"Some jokes were then passed about the apparent defection of Robertson from his spouse, and the meeting concluded their business without him, his party being exceedingly annoyed at his absence, which they thought not fair to the cause.

"'He should have given us his support.'

"'I suppose he has altered his opinions.'

"'Then he had better have said so.'

"'It struck me, certainly, that he was rather lukewarm on the subject when I talked to him last night; but on Tuesday I saw him just before he started, and he said he would not miss the meeting on any account. I'll go and look after him and know what he means.'

"Accordingly, Brown proceeded to his friend's house, and found Mrs. Robertson and her children at dinner.

"'Weel," Mr. Brown,' she said, 'so your meeting's over.'

"'Aye,' said he, 'but where's Robertson? Why didn't he keep his word with us?'

"'Why, you see, I dare say he meant to be back-indeed, I know he did: but business won't be neglected, and I suppose he could not manage it.'

"'Do you mean to say he's not come back!' said Brown.

"'Sure, I do,' answered Mrs. R. 'Of course, he'd have been at the meeting if he had.'

"'But people saw him last night, standing at his own door,' answered the cautious Brown.

"'Na, na, Mr. Brown, don't you believe that,' said Mrs. R., laughing; they that say that had too much whiskey in their een.'

"The children laughed at the idea of anybody seeing their father when he was at Raasa, and on the whole it was evident, that if John Robertson had returned, it was unknown to his family. But what could be his reason for so strange a proceeding, and why, if he wanted to evade the meeting, had he needlessly shown himself at all? Why not really stay away from Portree?

"However, Robertson did not appear; and later in the day the landlord of the Tun said to Brown, as he was passing the door, 'You must have been mistaken about seeing Mr. Robertson; the boat from Raasa is not come in.'

"'Then he must have come over by some other, for I not only saw him but walked and talked with him. I can't think what he can mean by playing at Hide and Seek in this way?'

"'It's very extraordinary,' said the landlord, 'for I am expecting a hamper from Raasa; and so, hearing from you that Mr. Robertson was come, I went down to inquire about it; but they declare no boat of any sort has come in these two days; the wind's right against them.'

"'I know the boat from Raasa is not come back,' said the porter; 'for I saw Jenny McGill just now, and she says her husband is not returned.'

"'Really you'll persuade me that I'm not in my right senses,' said the perplexed Brown. 'If ever I saw Robertson in my life I saw him last night; I was going to call upon him, as he had asked me to do so before he went away; but I met him, not far from my own house; and what is more, he told me of a thing I did not know before, regarding a purchase he had made, and spoke of what he intended to do with it.'

"'It's most extraordinary,' said the landlord.

"'Eh, sirs,' said an old fishwife, who was standing by, 'I wish it may not be John Robertson's ghaist that ye saw, for the wind's sair agin them, and I'd a bad dream about Jamie McGill last night.'

"They all laughed; but this was the first suggestion of the sort that had been made; and though he would not confess it, Brown began to feel rather uncomfortable; the more so as several things were recalled to his memory that had not struck him at the time. He remembered that Robertson had avoided shaking hands with him, either on meeting or parting, as was his wont; he had even then been struck with the grave tone of his conversation, and with his choosing that particular moment for pressing on his friend's attention what did not appear to have any urgent interest at present. Then it occurred to him that he looked ill and sad-he had attributed this to fatigue; but now, putting everything together, he could not help feeling a considerable degree of uneasiness. He kept hovering about Robertson's house, and from that to the shore all day; went to bed at night quite nervous; and by the next afternoon the alarm had spread and become universal. It was not without cause.

"John Robertson never came back; the boat had been lost-how, was not known, as all on board had perished. However, Mr. Brown took upon himself to be the friend and guardian of the bereaved family; and the information he received in that melancholy interview he was enabled to turn much to the advantage of their circumstances."

"A very remarkable story," said I.

"Yes," answered Dr. W. "very remarkable indeed, if true."

"And is it not true," I said, "remember, we are upon honour; I should think it a very ill compliment if any one attempted to mystify us with an invented story."

"I did not invent it, I assure you," replied Dr. W.; "I give it you as it was given to me on the spot. If you ask me if I believe it, I can't say I do."

"Do you think the people who told you believed it?"

"They certainly appeared to do so."

"And did it seem generally believed?"

"I can't say but it did; but of course, one must have wonderfully strong evidence before one could believe such a thing as that."

"Granted; but unless you had seen the thing yourself, you cannot have stronger evidence of a phenomenon of that description, than that it was believed by those who had good reason to know the grounds of their belief. They were able to judge how far Mr. Brown was worthy of credit; and they had the advantage of having witnessed his demeanour at the public meeting, when he asserted that he had walked and talked with Robertson, at a time he could not possibly know if he was telling a lie, that the man would not sooner or later return to confute him. Besides, as far as we see, it would have been a useless and wicked lie, inasmuch as it was calculated to make the man's family very uneasy. His subsequent conduct does not at all countenance the persuasion that he was capable of such a proceeding.'

"Certainly not; but you know the Scotch are very superstitious."

"I can't agree with you; the higher and lower classes of the towns are exactly similar in that respect to the same classes of England. In all countries the lower classes are more disposed to put faith in these things, because they believe in their traditions and adhere to the axiom that seeing is believing. The higher classes, on the other hand, are carefully educated not to believe in such traditions and to reject the axiom that seeing is believing, if the thing seen is a ghost. Now I freely admit, that our senses often deceive us, and that we think we see what we do not; every body with the slightest intelligence has, I suppose, learnt to distrust his own senses to a certain extent; but why on one particular point we should reject their evidence altogether, I never could understand."

"You have heard, I suppose of spectral illusions?" said the Doctor.

"Of course I have, and admit their existence; but we have so many cases on our side, that doctrine will not cover, and it is so impossible for you to prove that any particular case of ghost seeing falls under that head, that it is no use discussing the subject. It complicates the difficulty I confess, but can never decide the question. I was going to say, however, that the shopkeepers and middle classes of Scotland are anything but what you mean by superstitious-the class to whom Brown and Robertson belong, is the most hardheaded, argumentative, and matter of fact in the kingdom; and their religion, which is eminently unimaginative, so far from inducing a belief in ghosts, would have a precisely opposite tendency, because ghosts do not form an article of belief in either the longer or shorter catechism. In the remoter districts of the Highlands, the people are said to have more of what you would call superstition; but the same peculiarity is remarked in all mountainous regions; and as it has never been satisfactorily accounted for, we will not enter into the discussion now."

Second Evening

"After the doctor's story, I fear mine will appear too trifling," said Mrs. M., "but as it is the only circumstance of the kind that ever happened to myself, I prefer giving it you to any of the many stories I have heard.

"About fifteen years ago, I was staying with some friends at a magnificent old seat in Yorkshire, and our host being very much crippled with the gout, was in the habit of driving about the park and neighbourhood in a low pony phaeton, on which occasions, I often accompanied him. One of our favourite excursions was to the ruins of an old abbey just beyond the park, and we generally returned by a remarkably pretty rural lane leading to the village, or rather, small town of C.

"One fine summer's evening we had just entered this lane, when seeing the hedges full of wild flowers, I asked my friend to let me alight and gather some; I walked on before the carriage picking honeysuckles and roses as I went along, till I came to a gate that led into a field. It was a common country gate, with a post on each side, and on one of these posts sat a large white cat, the finest animal of the kind I had ever seen; and as I have a weakness for cats, I stopt to admire this sleek, fat puss, looking so wonderfully comfortable in a very uncomfortable position; the top of the post on which it was sitting, with its feet doubled up under it, being out of all proportion to its body, for no Angola ever rivalled it in size.

"'Come on, gently,' I called to my friend, 'here's such a magnificent cat!' for I feared the approach of the phaeton would startle it away before he had seen it.

"'Where?' said he, pulling up his horse opposite the gate.

"'There,' said I, pointing to the post, 'Isn't it a beauty; I wonder if it would let me stroke it!'

"'I see no cat,' said he.

"'There on the post,' said I, but he declared he saw nothing, though puss sat there in perfect composure during this colloquy.

"'Don't you see the cat, James,' said I, in great perplexity to the groom.

"'Yes, ma'am; a large white cat on that post.'

"I thought my friend must be joking, or else losing his eye-sight, and I approached the cat, intending to take it in my arms, and carry it to the carriage; but as I drew near, she jumped off the post, which was natural enough-but to my surprise she jumped into nothing-as she jumped she disappeared! no cat in the field-none in the lane-none in the ditch!

"'Where did she go, James?'

"'I don't know, ma'am, I can't see her,' said the groom, standing up in his seat, and looking all round.

"I was quite bewildered; but still I had no glimmering of the truth; and when I got into the carriage again, my friend said he thought I and James were dreaming, and I retorted that I thought he must be going blind.

"I had a commission to execute as we passed through the town, and I alighted for that purpose at the little haberdasher's; and while they were serving me, I mentioned that I had seen a remarkably beautiful cat sitting on a gate in the lane; and asked if they could tell me who it belonged to, adding, it was the largest cat I ever saw.

"The owners of the shop, and two women who were making purchases, suspended their proceedings, looked at each other, and then looked at me, evidently very much surprised.

"'Was it a white cat, ma'am?' said the mistress.

"'Yes, a white cat; a beautiful creature and —'

"'Bless me!' cried two or three, 'the lady's seen the *White Cat of C.* It hasn't been seen these twenty years.'

"'Master wishes to know if you'll soon be done, ma'am? The pony is getting restless,' said James.

"Of course, I hurried out, and got into the carriage, telling my friend that the cat was well known to the people at C., and that it was twenty years old.

"In those days, I believe, I never thought of ghosts, and least of all should I have thought of the ghost of a cat; but two evenings afterwards, as we were driving down the lane, I again saw the cat in the same position, and again my companion could not see it, though the groom did. I alighted immediately, and went up to it. As I approached, it turned its head, and looked full towards me with its soft, mild eyes, and a kindly expression, like that of a loving dog; and then, without moving from the post, it began to fade gradually away, as if it were a vapour, till it had quite disappeared. All this the groom saw as well as myself; and now there could be no mistake as to what it was. A third time, I saw it in broad daylight, and my curiosity greatly awakened, I resolved to make further inquiries amongst the inhabitants of C., but before I had an opportunity of doing so, I was summoned away by the death of my eldest child, and I have never been in that part of the world since. However, I once mentioned the circumstance to a lady who was acquainted with that neighbourhood, and she said she had heard of the White Cat of C., but had never seen it.

"But as you may not think this story very interesting since it only relates to a cat, I will, if you please, tell you another, in which I was concerned, although I saw nothing myself."

"We shall be very happy," I said, "but I am far from thinking your story wanting in interest, in fact, to me it has a very peculiar interest. There are few friends so sincere as the animals who have loved us, and none that I, for my part, more earnestly desire to see again. I have had two dogs, in my life, who contributed much to my happiness while they lived, and never caused me a sorrow till they died. Besides, there is a deep mystery in the being of these creatures, which proud man never seeks to unravel, or condescends to speculate on. What is their relation to the human race? Why are these spiritual germs embodied in those forms and made subject to man, that hard and cruel master! who assumes to be their superior, because he is endowed with some higher faculties, the most of which he grossly misuses. How beautiful are their characters when studied? how wonderful their intelligence when cultivated? how willing they are to serve us when kindly treated? But man, by his cruelty, ignorance, laziness, and want of judgment, spoils their temper, blunts their intelligence, deteriorates their nature, and then punishes them for being what he himself has made them. Well might Chalmers exclaim, 'All nature groans beneath the cruelty of man.' Why are these creatures, sinless, as far as we see, placed here as the subjects of this barbarous, unthinking tyrant? That has always appeared to me a solemn question."

After this little digression, Mrs. M. continued as follows: —

"I had been travelling on the continent, and was staying at Brussels on my way home. The bedroom I occupied was within another, in which slept my faithful maid, Rachel, and one of my children. I had been in bed sometime, and had not been to sleep, when I heard Rachel's voice, saying something which I did not distinctly hear, and before I could ask what it was, she uttered a cry that immediately brought me to her bedside. I found her in a state of violent agitation, and as soon as she was composed enough to speak, she told me that she had not been long in bed when she heard a voice call her, which she supposed to be mine, and immediately afterwards, in the glass which was opposite the foot of the bed, she saw a figure in white, enter and proceed to the other end of the room. She concluded it was me in my night dress, and that I had only mentioned her name to ascertain if she was awake, fearing to disturb the child, who was restless, she lay still, and did not answer. The figure went back through the door, but presently returned again, and seemed to be looking about for something, whereupon she half sat up in bed; when it approached, and laid its hand heavily on her knee, there was something painful in the pressure, and she exclaimed, 'Oh, don't do that ma'am!' but she had scarcely uttered the words when she discerned the features, and saw it was her sister. The phantom looked sadly at her, and then retreating to the opposite corner, disappeared. This circumstance, in spite of my arguments and suggestions that it was a dream, made a very painful impression on her; she felt sure some misfortune had happened, and so it proved; her sister had died on that night, leaving a family of young children, about whom, in her last moments, she was very anxious."

"Cases of that sort are very numerous," said Lady A., "I know of two which I can give upon perfectly good authority. A friend of mine was sitting a few years since in the drawing room at her country seat; there was a door at each end, leading to other rooms, both of which were open. A slight rustle caused her to raise her eyes from her work, when she saw her nephew enter at one door, walk straight through, and out at the other. The young man was at college, and she had no reason to expect him then, but concluding some unforeseen business had brought him, and that he was in search of her, she called —'Arthur, here I am,' and pursued him into the adjoining room, and then into the hall. Receiving no answer, and not being able to find him in any direction, she rang for the servants, and inquired where he was; but they did not know; they had seen nothing of him. She insisted he had arrived, and he was sought for all over the house and grounds in vain. The thing remained perfectly incomprehensible, till the post brought a letter, announcing that the young man had been drowned on that day.

"Another instance, equally well established, is that of Dr. C., of Dublin. He resided with his family some few miles from the city, I believe, at or near Howth, and when he returned in the evening after visiting his patients, he frequently, to save time, took a short cut across some sands, which in certain states of the tide were not always safe. Mrs. C. had often entreated him to relinquish this practice, and take the more circuitous way; but he thought he was too well acquainted with the place to run any danger. One evening that they were expecting him, as usual, to dinner, his brother, who was standing at the window, saw him arrive; he rode a white horse, and was therefore a conspicuous object. When the dinner hour came, as he had not appeared in the drawing room, his brother and Mrs. C., to whom the latter had mentioned having seen him, desired the servants to seek him in his dressing room, and ask if he was ready. He was not in his room, nor was he any where to be found; neither had any of the servants seen him, nor was his horse in the stable. Mr. C., however, confident of his arrival, suggested that he might be gone to visit some sick person in the neighbourhood; so they waited. But in vain; news presently arrived that horse and man had been drowned that evening in crossing the sands."

There was scarcely any one present unacquainted with examples of this kind of appearance amongst their family or friends, but Captain L. related to us a case still more curious and unaccountable that had happened to himself in India when he was in the Himalaya.

"I was just finishing my breakfast one morning," said he, "when my servant entered and announced a visitor. It was Captain P. B. of ours, who came to invite me to a game of billiards. Our billiard-room was situated about a mile beyond my quarter, and Captain B., who lived at the other extremity, had to pass my residence to go to it.

"'Are you going up there now?' I said.

"'Yes,' said he; 'will you come?'

"'Why, I can't come directly,' I answered; 'for I have a letter to write first; but if you'll go on, I'll join you presently.'

"He left me, and as soon as I had written my letter, I started for the billiard-room. When I entered it, Captain P. B. was not there, nor, indeed, anybody but the marker-which was not surprising, as it was earlier than we usually went there.

"'Where's Captain B?' I said.

"'Don't know, sir; he has not been here yet.'

"'Not been here?'

"'No, sir, not to-day.'

"Thinking, that as I was not ready, he had filled up the interval by going somewhere else, I began knocking about the balls; every now and then looking out of the window, expecting to see him approach; but when this had lasted upwards of two hours, I began to be rather impatient, and was just thinking of going away, when I saw him approaching with his wife in an open carriage from an opposite direction.

"'A pretty fellow you are, to keep me kicking my heels here waiting for you,' said I, as he entered the room.

"'Keep you waiting!' he said; 'I have not kept you waiting.'

"'Why, I've been here these two hours and more.'

"'How was I to know that; I did not know you were coming up here.'

"'Why, I told you I'd come as soon as I had finished my letter.'

"'My dear fellow, what are you talking about?' exclaimed my friend, in evident surprise; 'when did you tell me so? I don't recollect making any appointment to meet you to-day.'

"'What! not this morning, as you were passing my quarter?' said I, amazed in my turn. 'Didn't you ask me to come and play a game at billiards; and didn't I tell you I'd come as soon as I had finished my letter? and I did.'

"P. B. looked at me as if he thought I'd suddenly become insane; but as I suppose my countenance did not confirm that impression, he said, 'Here's some mistake; when do you suppose I made this appointment with you?'

"'Suppose!' I answered, rather indignant; 'what do you mean by *suppose*? Didn't you come into my quarter about three hours ago, just as I was finishing breakfast, and ask me to come up here and play a game at billiards with you?'

"'No; it must have been somebody else. Who gave you the message?'

"'Message! there was no message,' I answered, quite bewildered. 'You came in yourself-you know you did. What's the use of trying to hoax one?'

"'I don't know whether you are trying to hoax *me*,' replied P. B.; 'but upon my soul I have not been in your quarter to-day; nor have I seen you at all, till I entered this room. Moreover, I went with my wife at an early hour to breakfast with Captain D., and we are now returning thence; and I told the coachman to set me down here as he passed.'

"This was most confounding; and as we were both equally positive in what we asserted, we left the billiard-room together, and proceeded to take the testimony of my servant. On being asked who he had introduced when I was finishing breakfast, he unhesitatingly answered, Captain B. His account, in short, coincided entirely with mine.

"'Now then,' said Captain B., 'as you have your witness, you must hear mine,' and we went on to his quarter, where I received the most satisfactory and unimpeachable evidence, that what he said was correct. He had left home with Mrs. B. at six o'clock, and gone by appointment to breakfast with Captain D., who lived quite in a different direction to my quarter; and Captain D. afterwards testified to his never having left his house till he stept into the carriage with his wife.

"This event created a great sensation at the time; and people endeavoured by every means to explain it away, but nobody ever could. Captain B. did not like it at all; and his wife and family were very much alarmed, but nothing ensued, and I believe he is alive and well at this moment."

We next turned to Madame Von B., who said she knew so many cases of spiritual appearances, and occurrences of that nature, that she was rather perplexed by the abundance of her recollections. Amongst these she selected the following on account of its singularity: —

"We resided a great deal on the continent before I was married, and my mother had a favourite maid, called Françoise, who lived with her many years —a most trustworthy, excellent creature, in whom she had the greatest confidence; insomuch, that when I married, being very young and very inexperienced, as she was obliged to separate from me herself, she transferred Françoise to my service, considering her better able to take care of me than anybody else.

"I was living in Paris then, where Françoise, who was a native of Metz, had some relations settled in business, whom she often used to visit. She was generally very chatty when she returned from these people; for I knew all her affairs, and through her, all their affairs; and I took an interest in whatever concerned her or hers.

"One Sunday evening, after she had been spending the afternoon with this family, observing that she was unusually silent, I said to her, while she was undressing me, 'Well, Françoise, haven't you anything to tell me? How are your friends? Has Madame Pelletier got rid of her *grippe*?'

"Françoise started as if I had awakened her out of a reverie, and said, 'Oh! oui, Madame; oui, mercé; elle se porte bien aujourd'hui.'

"'And Monsieur Pelletier and the children, are they well?'

"'Oui, Madame, merci; ils se portent bien.'

"These curt answers were so unlike those she generally gave me, that I was sure her mind was pre-occupied, and that something had happened since we parted in the morning; so I turned round to look her in the face, saying *'Mais, qu'avez vous donc, Françoise? Qu'est ce qu'il y a?'*

"Then I saw what I had not observed before, that she was very pale, and that her cheeks had a glazed look, which showed that she had been crying.

"'Mais, ma bonne Françoise,' I said; 'vous avez quelque chose-est il arrivé quelque malheur à Metz?'

"'C'est cela, Madame,' answered Françoise, who had a brother there whom she had not seen for several years, but to whom she still continued affectionately attached. His name was Benoît, and he was in a good service as garde forestier to a nobleman who possessed very extensive estates, *près de chez nous*, as Françoise said. He had a wife and children; and some time before the period I am referring to, Françoise had told me, with great satisfaction, that in order to make him more comfortable, the Prince de M—— had given Benoît the privilege of gathering up all the dead wood in the forest to sell for firewood, which, as the estate was very large, rendered his situation extremely profitable. When she said 'c'est cela, Madame,' Françoise, who had just encased me in my dressing gown, sunk into a chair, and having declared that she was *bête, très bête*, she gave way to a hearty good cry, after which, being somewhat relieved, she told me the following strange story:—

"'You remember,' she said, 'that the prince was so good as to give Benoît all the dead wood of the forest-and a great thing it was for him and his family, as you will think, when I tell you it was worth upwards of two thousand francs a-year to him. In short, he was growing rich, and perhaps he was getting to think too much of his money and too little of the *bon Dieu* —at all events, this privilege which the prince gave him to make him comfortable, and which made him a great man amongst the foresters, has been the cause of a dreadful calamity.'

"'How?' said I.

"'We never heard anything of what had happened,' said she, till yesterday, when Mons. Pelletier received a letter from Benoît's wife, and another from a cousin of ours, relating what I am going to tell you, and saying that both he and his family had wished to keep it secret; but that was no longer possible.'

"'Well, and what has happened?'

"'La chose la plus incroyable! Eh bien, Madame; it appears that one day last autumn, Benoît went out in the forest to gather the dead-wood. He had his cart with him, and as he gathered it he bound it into faggots and threw it in the cart. He had extended his search this day to a remote part of the forest, and found himself in a spot he did not remember to have visited before; indeed, it was evident to him that he had not, or he could not have escaped seeing an old wooden cross which was lying on the ground, and had apparently fallen into that recumbent position from old age. It was such a cross as is usually set up where a life has been lost, whether by murder or suicide; or sometimes when poor wanderers are frozen to death or lost in the deep winter snows. He looked about for the grave, but saw no indication of one; and he tried to remember if any catastrophe had happened there in his time, but could recall none. He took up the cross and examined it. He saw that the wood was decayed, and it bore such marks of antiquity, that he had no doubt the person whose grave it had marked had died before he was born-it looked as if it might be a hundred years old.

"'Eh bien,' said Françoise, wiping her eyes, into which the tears kept starting, 'of course you will think that Benoît, or anybody in the world who had the fear of God before his eyes, as he could not find the grave to replace it as it should be, would have laid it reverently down where he had found it, saying a prayer for the soul of the deceased; but, alas! the demon of avarice tempted him, and he had not the heart to forego that poor cross, but bound it up into a faggot with the rest of the dead wood he found there, and threw it into his cart!'

"'Well, Françoise,' said I, 'you know I am not a Catholic, but I respect the custom of erecting these crosses, and I do think your brother was very wrong; I suppose he has lost the prince's favour by such impious greediness.'

"'Pire que ça! worse than that,' she replied. 'It appears that while he was committing this wicked action, he felt an extraordinary chill come over him, which made him think that, though it had been a mild day, the evening must have suddenly turned very cold, and hastily throwing the faggot into his cart, he directed his steps homeward. But walk as he would, he still felt this chill down his back, so that he turned his head to look where the wind blew from, when he saw, with some dismay, a mysterious-looking figure following close upon his footsteps. It moved noiselessly on, and was covered with a sort of black mantle that prevented his discerning the features. Not liking its appearance, he jumped into the cart and drove home as fast as he could, without looking behind him; and when he got into his own farmyard he felt quite relieved, particularly, as when he alighted he saw no more of this unpleasant-looking stranger. So he began unloading his cart, taking out the faggots, one by one, and throwing them upon the ground; but when he threw down the one that contained the cross, he received a blow upon his face, so sharp that made him stagger and involuntarily shout aloud. His wife and children were close by, but there was no one else to be seen; and they would have disbelieved him and fancied he had accidentally hit himself with the faggot, but that they saw the distinct mark on his cheek of a blow given with an open hand. However, he went into supper perplexed and uncomfortable; but when he went to bed this fearful phantom stood by his side, silent and terrible, visible to him, but invisible to others. In short, madame, this awful figure haunted him till, in spite of his shame, he resolved to consult our cousin Jerome about it.'

"But Jerome laughed, and said it was all fancy and superstition. 'You got frightened at having brought away this poor devil's cross, and then you fancy he's haunting you,' said he.

"But Benoît declared that he had thought nothing about the cross, except that it would make fire wood, and that he had no more believed in ghosts than Jerome; 'but now,' said he, 'something must be done. I can get no sleep and am losing my health; if you can't help me, I must go to the priest and consult him.'

"'Why don't you take back the cross and put it where you found it,' said Jerome.

"'Because I am afraid to touch it and dare not go to that part of the forest.'

"'So Jerome who did not believe a word about the ghost, offered to go with him and replace the cross. Benoît gladly accepted, more especially, as he said he saw the apparition standing even then beside him, apparently, listening to the conversation. Jerome laughed at the idea; however, Benoît lifted the cross reverently into the cart and away they went into the forest. When they reached the spot, Benoît pointed out the tree under which he had found it; and as he was shaking and trembling, Jerome took up the cross and laid it on the ground, but as he did so he received a violent blow from an invisible hand, and at the same moment saw Benoît fall to the ground. He thought he had been struck too, but it afterwards appeared that he had fainted from having seen the phantom with its upraised hand striking his cousin. However, they left the cross and came away; but there was an end to Jerome's laughter, and he was afraid the apparition would now haunt him. Nothing of the sort happened; but poor Benoît's health has been so shaken by this frightful occurrence that he cannot get the better of it; his friends have advised change of scene, and he is coming to Paris next week.'

"This was the story Françoise told me, and in a few days I heard he had arrived and was staying with Mons. Pelletier; but the shock had been too great for his nerves, and he died shortly after. They assured me that previous to that fatal expedition into the forest, he had been a hale, hearty man, totally exempt from superstitious fancies of any sort; and in short, wholly devoted to advancing his worldly prosperity and getting money."

Third Evening

"I don't know that I could tell you anything interesting in the way of Ghost Stories; I have never attended to them, though I have heard a great many," said Colonel C.; "but I can tell you an extraordinary circumstance which may, perhaps, be considered of a spiritual nature, and which I can myself vouch for the truth of.

"My father, when I was young, resided in the South of England —I shall not give the name of the place, nor of the people immediately concerned, if these stories are to be published; because, for anything I know, some persons may survive to whom the publication might give pain; I lived there with him and my mother and sisters. Our house was on the road between two large towns, situated about eight miles distant from each other; and though we had a little ground and a short avenue in front, we were not more than half a quarter of a mile from the highway. When all was still, we could distinctly hear the carts and carriages as they passed, and even distinguish by the sound of the wheels what kind of vehicle it was. There was a carrier that plied between these two towns, whom I will call Healy, and as everything we used we had from B., he was generally at our house three or four times a week; in short, he did our marketings, in a great degree; my mother giving him an order, as he passed, for what he was to bring back; and many a time Healy has smuggled a novel from the circulating library for my sisters, or done little commissions for me that I could not so well manage for myself. All this made him a popular character with us, for he was very obliging; but for all that, he did not bear the best of characters. It was his interest to be well with us, and the gentry in general, who were his customers; and he understood that too well to incur our ill-will; but by his equals and inferiors he was looked upon with a less favourable eye. They had nothing very positive to allege against him; but they thought him a hard, griping, greedy man, who was honest in his dealings with us because the slightest suspicion would have ruined his trade, but who would take an advantage when he thought no possible damage to himself could accrue from it. He was about forty years of age; tall, with a long face, prominent nose, and dark complexion; his shoulders were round, but his frame was wiry, and he was reputed very strong.

"One evening, between thirty and forty years ago, towards the beginning of winter, we were expecting Healy-my mother was solicitous about some provisions she had ordered for an approaching dinner-party; and I was very anxious for the arrival of a cricket-bat that I wanted for use the day after the next. Of course, long before the time he usually arrived, I was looking out for him, and fancying him late; I said, 'I wondered Healy was not come!' Upon which my father looked at his watch, and found that it wanted full half-an-hour of his time, which was nine o'clock; sometimes, indeed, later, but never earlier. It was then exactly half-past eight; and before my father had returned his watch into his pocket, one of my sisters exclaimed, 'Here he is!' and we heard the wheels coming up the avenue-we should have heard him before, but two of my sisters were practising a duet, which was to be produced at the approaching festivity, and drowned the sound.

"Thereupon, I and my mother left the room, and went towards the back door, where Healy had just alighted, and was bringing sundry packages into the kitchen.

"'Have you got my bat, Healy?' said I.

"'No, sir,' he replied; 'there wasn't one in the whole town the size you wanted; but I'll bring you one from S. as I pass to-morrow. I know they've got 'em there. I believe that's all, Ma'am?' he added, addressing my mother.

"She said she believed it was, and was going to pay him his week's account, which she had asked for, but he hurried out, saying, 'Another time, if you please, Ma'am; I'm rather late to-night;' and he was in his cart and away before I had time to give him some directions in regard to the bat.

"'What a hurry he's in!' I said; 'and it wants almost twenty minutes to nine now.'

"'I suppose he has a great many places to stop at,' said my mother; 'if he don't get all his parcels delivered before people are gone to bed, he gets into trouble sometimes. He's a very punctual fellow certainly.'

"We returned to the drawing-room, and resumed our occupations; and about half-an-hour afterwards-happening to be all silent at the moment, we heard a pair of light wheels and a brisk trotting horse passing in the road.

"'That's farmer Gould's mare, I'm sure,' said I. 'What a famous trotter she is!'

"'Yes,' said my father; 'I wish he'd part with her. I made him an offer the other day. I should like her for my buggy.'

"'And what did he say? Won't he sell her?'

"'He said nothing-he only laughed, and shook his fat sides.'

"'Money is no object to him,' said my mother, 'he won't part with her unless he gets another he likes better.'

"We breakfasted at nine o'clock, and I was getting up, and about half dressed, when one of my sisters burst into my room, crying, 'La! Fred., such a shocking thing has happened! poor Farmer Gould was found dead in the road this morning; they think his horse ran away, for it's not to be found; and the chaise was upset and lying on its side. How lucky, papa did not get the mare!'

"'Who says so?' said I.

"'The postman;' she answered, 'he saw some labourers standing round something in the road; and when he came up to them, he found it was the chaise, and poor farmer Gould quite dead beside it!'

"When I got down stairs I found the whole house occupied with the subject of this sad accident, all lamenting the good man, who was a general favourite, and agreeing that, for so heavy a person, a two-wheeled carriage was very dangerous, as a fall was almost sure to be fatal.

"My father said when he had finished his letters and papers he would walk up to the farm, and see if he could be of any use to poor Mrs. Gould; I, with the curiosity of fifteen, begged to go with him; and my mother improved the occasion by giving the governor a serious lecture about his love for high-trotting horses and buggies.

"I expected Healy with my bat about eleven o'clock, as he had nothing else to bring, I knew he wouldn't come up the avenue, but leave it at a cottage near our gate; and wishing to learn if he'd heard any particulars about the accident, I walked down to meet him when the hour approached. Presently, I saw him coming, sitting in front of his cart.

"'Well, Healy,' I said, 'isn't this a shocking thing about poor Farmer Gould? You've heard he was found dead in the road this morning?'

"'Yes, Sir, the mare ran away, and pitched him out upon his head; I can't say as ever I liked her myself; but I've got your bat, Master Frederick; a nice un too; I wouldn't come away this morning till I'd got it.'

"I thanked him, and he drove on, as if he had no time to lose in gossip, while I was untying the string of my parcel.

"By the time my father and I reached Gould's farm, the doctor had arrived from B., and we heard he was examining the body in the parlour, where it had been laid by the labourers who found it. The chaise, too, was standing near the door, just as it had been wheeled up, and the mare, they told us, had been found in a neighbouring field, with the harness hanging about her, and unhurt, except on the forehead, where she appeared to have had a violent blow. The farm men, standing about, said, that she had no doubt taken her head, and ran foul of something, and so pitched out Mr. Gould, and overturned the chaise; which seemed likely enough.

"My father said, he should like to see Mr. Wills, the surgeon; so we stood about outside till he came. When he did, he looked very grave, as, indeed, befitted the occasion; but in answer to my father's inquiries, he said, that he could give no decided opinion of the cause of death till he had investigated the case further; and then he proceeded to examine the chaise, and next the horse. He then walked with us down to the spot where the thing had happened, and narrowly surveyed the ground; but he was very uncommunicative, which, as we knew him well, rather surprised us. He hurried away, saying, that he must prepare for the inquest on the following day.

"My father went to the inquest; and I should have liked to go, too, but I was engaged to play a match at cricket with a few of my young neighbours. However, I was home first, for the inquest lasted a long time, and took a very unexpected turn.

"It appeared that Mr. Wills, who was by marriage a connexion of Gould's wife, had suspected on the first examination of the body that the farmer had not come fairly by his end. It so happened that Gould had dined with him the last day he was at B., and had mentioned to him that he had 'at last got that seventy pounds that he was afraid he should never see;' alluding to some money that had been long owing to him; and as he spoke, he drew from his pocket a bundle of notes, some of which appeared to be of the Bank of England, and some of country banks. As soon, therefore, as Wills had arrived at certain conclusions, he inquired of Mrs. Gould if she had found his money safe.

"In her grief and surprise it had not occurred to her to search-and indeed she was not aware of his having any sum of importance about him. They proceeded immediately to examine his pockets, but no notes were there; a few shillings, a silver watch, and some unconsidered trifles, were all that was found about him. Mr. Wills made inquiries at the banker's and others, at B., and by the time the inquest sat he was prepared to say, that there was every reason to think that Mr. Gould had had this money in his waistcoat pocket, where he had seen him deposit it, at the time he left to return home.

"This presented quite a new view of the case to the coroner, who had come there without the slightest suspicion of anything beyond an accident. The labourers were examined as to the attitude in which they had discovered the body, which, they all agreed, was lying on its face; and indeed there were some stains from the dirt of the road, which testified to this being the case; yet, according to Mr. Wills, death had been occasioned by a terrible blow on the back of the head which had fractured the skull; and which, in his opinion, was inflicted by a heavy bludgeon. The man's hair was very thick behind; but on dividing it a wound was visible, from which a small quantity of blood had oozed and dried up.

"After a long investigation, the inquest was adjourned for a few days in order that further evidence might be collected. We were all much excited about this affair; it formed the staple of conversation at our dinner party, and various were the conjectures formed as to who was the criminal, if criminal there were; for some thought it possible that Gould had fallen on his back in the first instance, and then got upon his legs, and fallen a second time on his face; but Mr. Wills was confident the death wound was not the result of a fall; and besides, where was the money? Then all agreed, that if he had been robbed, it was by no ordinary thief; it must have been by some one who knew the sum he had in his pocket, and who did not care for the loose silver and the watch.

"'No doubt,' said my father, 'they will find out if anybody was present when the money was paid to him, or he may have told somebody of it, as he told Wills.'

"We had so many things provided for the party, that for two or three days we wanted nothing of Healy and did not see him; but the servants having mentioned that they wanted soap for the next week's washing, my mother sent a note to the cottage, where he always stopt to enquire for orders, desiring him to bring some on his return, and also a barrel of beer for the use of the kitchen.

"When I heard the cart coming up the avenue, I went to the back door, to have a little gossip.

"'Well Healy,' said I, as he rolled in the barrel of beer; have you heard any news?'

"'No sir,' said he.

"'Nothing about farmer Gould?' I asked.

"'No sir, nothing. Shall I put the beer in the cellar?' he enquired.

"This question being answered, I said, 'Did you meet anybody on the road that night?'

"'Lord, sir, I meet loads of people as I never take any notice of. I've enough to do to mind my own business.'

"'You couldn't have been far off when he was attacked-for you know Mr. Wills says he's been killed by a blow on the back of the head, don't you?'

"'Well, sir, I've heard so; but how should he know? He wasn't there, I suppose. Anything else wanted, sir?'

"'I believe not, Healy,' I said; and he got into his cart and drove away while I went back to the drawing-room.

"'What does Healy say?' asked my father. 'Has he heard anything new about this affair?'

"'No, he says he hasn't, but he said very little and seemed rather sulky, I thought.'

"'By the bye, he couldn't have been far off when the thing happened; for he had only been gone half-an-hour when we recognized the step of poor Gould's mare I recollect, and she'd soon overtake him.'

"'So I told him; and I asked him if he had met anybody on the road that night, but he said he'd plenty to do to mind his own business.'

"My father who was reading the paper at the time, looked up at me over his spectacles; and then fell into a reverie that lasted some minutes, but he said nothing; my mother observed that she thought Healy ought to be summoned as a witness; and my father rejoined, that no doubt he'd be examined.

"On the following day the inquest was resumed; my father went early and had some private conversation with Mr. Wills and I waited outside amongst the assembled crowd, listening to their speculations and conjectures. Presently, the coroner arrived, and I went in with him and heard the whole of the evidence. That of Mr. Wills, and the labourers who found the body was the same as before. Then, as my father had conjectured, Healy was called; his face was familiar to everybody in the room, and there was not one I should think who was not struck with the singularly sulky, dogged expression his features had assumed. There was no manifest reason for it, for he was only summoned like other witnesses, and no breath of suspicion had been cast upon him; at least, as far as we had heard. But he evidently came in a spirit of resistance and wound up for self-defence. He declared that he had not overtaken Mr. Gould on the night in question, and did not know he was on the road; nor did he hear anything of what had happened till the next morning. He believed he had met some tramps on the road that night-two men and a woman-but he had not particularly noticed them, and he did not recollect meeting anybody else. He had first heard of the accident at a shop where he had gone to buy a bat for Master C. When he said this, he looked up at me and our eyes met. I have often thought of that look since.

"The next witness was Mr. F., who had paid Gould the seventy pounds in notes; and then a Mr. H. B., a solicitor, came forward and volunteered the following evidence, which, he said, he should have given before, but that he had left home on the afternoon preceding this unfortunate business, and had only returned yesterday. He was acquainted with Gould; and had met him at the door of the bank at B ——, as he himself was on his way to the coach that was starting for E. Gould spoke to him, and said he had just got that seventy pounds; and when he said so, he clapt his hand on his pocket, implying it was there. He said, 'I came to pay it in here, but I see they're shut, and it does not signify; I shall have to pay away a good deal of it next week;' this was all that passed, as I told him I must be off for I should lose the coach. Upon this, he was asked if anybody else had been present when Gould made this communication. He answered, that people had been passing to and fro, but he could not say whether they heard it. There was one person who he thought might, though he could not affirm that he did; and that was Healy, the carrier, who was standing at the door of the tanner's shop, which is next to the bank, and examining some cricket bats that he had in his hand. Gould had spoken loud, as was his wont.

"I saw Mr. Wills and my father exchange looks when this evidence was given, and then for the first time the question occurred to me, could Healy be the murderer? I could hardly entertain the suspicion-it is so difficult to believe such a thing of a person one is having constant intercourse with. Healy was recalled and asked if he remembered seeing Mr. Gould and the lawyer together on that day. He declared he did not.

"The harness was afterwards produced; and it appeared that the traces had been cut, which was a strong confirmation of the worst suspicions.

"The inquest was once more adjourned; and Healy plied his trade as usual for the next two days, though everybody had a strange feeling towards him; and he retained his dogged, sulky look; on the third night we missed him. We had expected a parcel from B — —, but he did not come; and the next day we heard he had been arrested on suspicion of being the murderer of Mr. Gould. A gentleman's servant, who had been out without leave to some festivity at B — —, and had come home and got in at the pantry window without being discovered, at last came forward, and said, that as he was going to the rendezvous, he had seen a cart, which he believed to be Healy's, though it was very dark, drawn right across the road; the horse was out of the shafts and tied to a gate, for he nearly ran against him; he did not see any person with the cart, but the driver might be behind it. It was just where there are some large trees over-hanging the road, which made it darker than in other parts; and a person driving would not see the obstruction till he was on it. He himself, thinking it was Healy, slipt quietly by, for he did not want to be recognised, as the carrier often came to his master's, and might have betrayed him. He met a one-horse carriage about a couple of miles further on; the horse was trotting pretty fast. He thought it was Mr. Gould, but he could not positively say, as the night was so dark.

"The spot described was precisely where Mr. Gould's body was found; and the man added, that it struck him when he met the gig, that if the cart had not moved out of the way, there would be an accident, and he should have warned the driver to look out, if he had not been upon a lark himself.

"You may imagine the sensation created by this allegation in the neighbourhood, where the carrier was so well known. Till the spring assizes at E — —, where he was to be tried, it furnished the staple of conversation, and every fresh bit of evidence, for or against him, was eagerly repeated and canvassed. My father was summoned as a witness to the hour at which Healy had been at our house that night, and also to the recognising the foot of Mr. Gould's mare. The evidence was entirely circumstantial, as nobody had witnessed the murder, though murder there certainly had been; nor was there anybody else to whom suspicion could attach. As for the tramps Healy said he had met, no trace of them could be found, nor did anyone appear to have seen such a party.

"When all the evidence had been heard, my father said he felt considerable doubt what the verdict would be, and he really believed the jury were greatly perplexed; but when Healy stood up, and in the most solemn manner said, 'I am innocent, my Lord! I call God to witness, I am innocent! May this right arm wither if I murdered the man!' So great an impression was made on the court, that, added to the prisoner's previous good character, every body saw he would be acquitted.

"He was; Healy went forth a free man, and we were all too glad to believe in his innocence, to dispute the justice of the verdict; but lo! the hand of the Lord was on him. He had called upon God to bear witness to his words; and he did. In three days from that time, Richard Healy's stalwart right arm was withered! The muscles shrunk; the skin dried up; and it looked like the limb of a mummy!

"Though a voice from Heaven testified against him, he could not be arraigned again for the same crime, and he remained at liberty. He attempted for a short time to carry on his business, but people ceased to employ him; and his feeble arm could no longer lift the boxes and hampers with which his cart was wont to be loaded. He went about, avoided by every one but his own immediate connexions. I often met him, but he never looked me in the face; indeed, he rarely, if ever, raised his eyes; his round shoulders grew rounder, till he came to stoop like an old man. He seemed to move under a heavy burthen that weighed him to the earth.

"After an interval, however, he bought some property; and in his old age-for he survived his trial several years-he was in prosperous circumstances. But everybody said, 'Where did he get the money?'

"We were all deeply interested in this singular story; and in reference to the withered arm, Colonel C. said, that he should certainly not have believed it had he not seen it himself.

"I think, said I, that it was not so difficult to account for the phenomenon as at first appears. Had he been innocent, the solemn adjuration he uttered in court would have been justifiable in the eyes of God and man, and would have occasioned him no concern afterwards; but he was guilty; he had called upon God to bear witness to a lie, and, doubtless, the consciousness of this sacrilegious appeal filled him with horror and alarm. He would tremble lest his prayer should be heard and the curse fall upon him. These terrors would direct all his thoughts to his arm, and produce the very thing he feared; for Sir Henry Holland asserts that the mind is capable of acting upon the body to such a degree, as sometimes to create disease in a particular part on which the attention is too intently fixed."

Fourth Evening

"The circumstance I am going to mention," said Sir Charles L., "will appear very insignificant after these interesting narratives, but as it happened very lately, you'll perhaps think it worth hearing.

"I was living a few months ago in an hotel, the owner of which died while I was there. He had an apoplectic seizure, and expired shortly afterwards. A week before this happened, at a time he was supposed to be in perfect health, an acquaintance of the family called, and without giving any reason, requested his daughter not to attend a ball she was engaged to go to. The young lady did not take her advice; but the visitor confided to another person that she had a particular reason for her request, which reason was as follows: —

"The night before she called, she and her husband had retired to bed in a somewhat anxious state of mind respecting a near relative of theirs, who was very ill, and whom they had been visiting. The husband, however, soon fell asleep, but the wife lay thinking of the sick person, and the consequences that would ensue if she died, when her reflections were interrupted by seeing a bright spot of light suddenly appear upon the wall-that is, upon the wainscoat of her room. She looked about to see whence it proceeded; there was no light burning, nor could any be reflected from the window; as she looked it increased in size, till, at last, it was as large as the frame of a picture; then there began to appear in the frame a form, gradually developed, till there was a perfect head and face, hair and all, distinctly visible.

"Whilst this development was proceeding, she lay, as it were, transfixed; she wanted to wake her husband, but she could neither speak nor move; at length she seemed to burst the bonds, and cried to him to look, but as she spoke, the vision faded, and by the time he was sufficiently aroused there was nothing to be seen.

"Both he and she interpreted this occurrence into a bad omen for their sick relative, and augured very ill of her case; but the next morning, as she was standing in her shop, she saw the hotel keeper pass to market, and he nodded to her, whereupon she turned to her husband, and exclaimed —'That's the face I saw last night! Sure nothing can be going to happen to him!'

"I heard these circumstances from my servant; and the unexpected seizure and death occurred within a few days."

"When I was at Weimar, about two years ago," said Mademoiselle G., "an accident occurred that occupied the attention of the whole place, and which seems to belong to the same class of phenomena as the story just related. The palace, called the Château, in Weimar, is at one end of the park, and at the other end is another château, called the Belvedere; both are ducal residences, and an avenue runs from the one palace to the other. Opposite this avenue is the Russian chapel or Greek church-the present Dowager Duchess being a sister of the Emperor Nicholas-and in front of this chapel a sentinel is always posted.

"The Grand Duke, Charles Frederick, father of the present sovereign, was, at the period I allude to, residing at the Belvedere not well in health, but by no means alarmingly ill, for had that been the case he would have been brought into Weimar, where etiquette requires that the sovereign should make his first and last appearance in this world-there he must be born, and there die, if possible.

"One night the sentinel, who was standing at the entrance of the Russian chapel, was surprised to see, in the far distance, a long procession winding its way down the avenue from the Belvedere. As there was no stir in the town, for the night was far advanced, and as he had not heard of any solemnity in preparation, the man stared at it in mute wonder, but his amazement was redoubled when it approached near enough for him to distinguish the individual objects to perceive that it was a State funeral, accompanied by the royal mourners, and all the pomp usual at these ceremonies; the velvet pall bore the initials and arms of the duke, and following the bier was his favourite and well known horse, led by one of his attendants. Slowly and mournfully the procession moved on till it reached the chapel; the doors opened to admit the cortege; it passed in; and as the doors closed on this mysterious vision the soldier fell to the ground, where he was found in a state of insensibility when the guard was relieved.

"Of course, nobody believed his story; he was placed under arrest, severely punished, and had a nervous fever that brought him to the brink of the grave.

"I was there when this happened, said Mademoiselle G., and it was the talk of the town; almost everybody laughed at him; but five days afterwards the Duke fell suddenly ill, and was found to be in so dangerous a state, that the physicians forbade his being removed into the town. He finally died at the Belvedere, and was buried in the Russian chapel, exactly in the manner pourtrayed by the shadowy forms seen by the sentinel, and there buried."

We all agreed that these rehearsals, if we may so call them, are amongst the most perplexing of these very perplexing phenomena; a very curious case of this description will be found in one of the letters inserted in the Appendix.

"My sister-in-law, Lady S.," said Lady R., "Told me, the other day, that during her late residence in St. Petersburg, she was intimately acquainted with a Prussian lady of high rank, to whom the following strange events occurred, an account of which she herself gave to my sister. This Prussian lady was sitting one morning in her boudoir, when she heard a rustling sound in the ante-room, which was divided by a *portière* from the boudoir. The sound continuing, she rose and drew aside the curtain to ascertain the cause, when, to her surprise, she saw a very pale man, in a Chasseur's uniform, standing in the middle of the room. She was about to speak to him, and inquire what he was doing there, when he retreated towards the window and vanished. Greatly alarmed, she sought her husband, and related what had occurred; but he laughed at her, and desired her not to expose herself to ridicule by talking of it. Some days afterwards, whilst in the boudoir, she heard the same rustling noise near her, and on looking up, she saw the figure of the Chasseur suspended in the air between the ceiling and the floor, with his legs dangling in the air. A scream brought her husband, who was in the adjoining room, and he saw the figure as well as herself. Nevertheless, the fear of ridicule kept them silent; but some time afterwards, when they had a party, one of the company exclaimed, 'Good Heavens! This, I remember, is the very room that unfortunate Chasseurs hung himself in!' And then they learned that the house had been previously occupied by the Danish minister, and that a Chasseur in his service had, from some cause or other, committed suicide."

"I don't know whether dreams are admissible," said Miss M.; "but the sort of occurrences just related appear to me to be little removed from waking dreams. I know two cases of extraordinary dreaming, the authenticity of which I can answer for, if you would like to hear them." We accepted gladly, and the lady began as follows: —

"My father was intimate with Mr. S. —whose name, perhaps, is known to you as the particular friend of Mr. Spencer Percival. This gentleman, Mr. S., when he was a young man, had one night a remarkable dream, that he could not in any way account for-the circumstances having no relation to any previous event, train of thought, or conversation whatever.

"He found himself, in his dream, on horseback, in a very extensive forest; he was alone, evening was drawing on, and he sought some place where he could pass the night. After riding a little farther, he espied an inn; he rode up to it and alighted, asking if they could give him lodging for the night, and stabling for his horse. They said 'yes,' and conducted him to an upper chamber. He ordered some refreshments, when it occurred to him that he should like to see how his horse was faring; and he descended, in order to find his way to the stables; in doing so, he got a glimpse of some very ill-looking men in a side chamber, who seemed in close conference; moreover, he thought he saw weapons lying on the table, and there were other circumstances which I do not precisely remember, the effect of which was to create alarm, and lead him to suspect he had fallen into a *repaire de voleurs*.

"He saw his horse rubbed down and fed, and then re-ascended to take his refreshment; betraying no suspicion of evil, but secretly resolved on flight. After his supper, he went down again, stood at the door, and pretended to stroll about. When he saw an opportunity, he went round to the stable, saddled his horse, and cautiously rode away. But he had not gone far, when he heard the tramp of horses' feet behind him, and from the pace they came, he felt sure he was pursued. He urged his horse forward, but the animal was not fresh-he had done his day's work already, and the pursuers were gaining on him, when he saw he was approaching a spot where two roads met. Which of the two should he follow? He had nothing to guide him in his choice, and his life probably depended on his decision! Suddenly, a voice whispered in his ear, 'Take the right!' He did so, and shortly reached a house where he obtained shelter and protection.

"When he awoke, the circumstances of his dream were so vividly impressed on his mind, that he could hardly believe the thing had not actually happened. He related it to his friends; and, for some days, thought a good deal of it; but he was just entering into active life, and the impression soon faded before the varied interests that absorbed him; and the strange dream was entirely forgotten.

"Many years afterwards, when he had reached middle age, he was travelling in Germany, and in the course of an excursion he was making to see the country, he had occasion to cross a part of the Schwarzwald-the Black Forest. He was on horseback and alone; he reached an inn, the aspect of which he fancied was familiar to him. Here he thought he might conveniently pass the night; so he alighted, ordered his supper, and then went to see his horse fed. On further acquaintance with the place, he did not like the look of it, and he saw suspicious-looking men hanging about. He resolved to seek another resting-place; and leaving some money on the table to pay for what he had had, he went down stairs, and after lounging about a little, strolled to the stable, saddled his horse, and rode off as quietly as he could. But he was missed and pursued, he heard the tramp of the horses as they gained upon him. At this critical moment, he saw he was approaching a place where the roads divided; his life depended on which of the two he should take; suddenly, and strange to say, though he had misty recollections of the scene, now for the first time, the dream of his youth clearly and vividly recurred to him. He remembered the voice that whispered, 'Take the right!' He obeyed the hint, and his pursuers soon gave up the chase. He found a château about half-a-mile from the turning; the owner of which hospitably received him. His host said there had been for some time unpleasant suspicions with regard to the inn in question; and that, if he had taken the left hand road, he would have been quite at their mercy."

This very curious dream reminded us of that of Dr. W., which I have related in the "Night Side of Nature;" who in the same manner was saved from the attack of an infuriated bull, in his dream, having been shown where to fly for safety; but the case is less remarkable than that of Mr. S., as the dream occurred only the night before the danger presented itself.

"The other dream I alluded to," said Miss M., "is less curious on that account. Some friends of mine, who reside in the country, had an old nurse who had lived in the family many years, and for whom they had a great regard. When her services ceased to be required, she was settled in a cottage on the estate, where she lived very comfortably with her only daughter. The daughter, however, married a man who kept a turnpike some miles distant; and one morning, just as the family were leaving home on some expedition, the old woman arrived in considerable agitation, saying that she had had a frightful dream about her daughter, and that she was going off immediately to the place where she lived. The ladies endeavoured to dissuade her from walking all that way, merely on account of a dream. But she said she could not rest, and must go. They even promised that if she would wait till the following day they would drive her there in the carriage, in which there was now no room; if there had been they would have taken her, as their road lay not far from the spot.

"With this offer they left her and went their way; but her anxiety would not permit her to wait; and shortly afterwards she set off and walked all the distance to the turnpike. The moment she arrived she saw reason to rejoice in her determination; she found her daughter alone, her husband having been called away on business; and, said the young woman, I am dreadfully alarmed, for there is a quantity of money in the house. The farmers are accustomed to bring the money for their rent here twice a year, as it save them several miles, and the agent always comes to fetch it on the same day. But a letter to my husband has just arrived from the agent to say, he can't come till to-morrow. Knowing his hand, I opened it; and I am terrified, for the custom of leaving the money here is no secret; and if it should get wind that it has not been fetched away, heaven knows what may happen.

"The old woman then told her daughter that she had dreamed on the preceding night that some thieves had broken into the turnpike house, and robbed and murdered the inhabitants.

"But what were these two helpless women to do, mutually confirmed in their apprehensions as they naturally were? It was already late in the day; there was no help near at hand, and besides they did not dare to separate in search of any. They watched anxiously for a traveller, resolved to confide in the first respectable one that passed, and beg him to send assistance. But none came that they thought it safe to trust. Night approached; and it being a little frequented road, except on market days, every moment their hope of help declined. So they did the best they could in this extremity; they shut and barricaded the lower part of the house, stopping up the door and windows with every piece of furniture they had, and locked themselves up, with the money, in an upper chamber, put out the light, and with a chink of the window open, they set themselves down to listen for the marauders whom they confidently expected to arrive.

"Nor were they disappointed; about eleven o'clock their anxious ears distinguished the sound of approaching footsteps. Presently, they heard voices and the door was attempted; the men said they had lost their way, and on receiving no answer they attempted to force an entrance. Then, the poor women knowing their poor defences would soon yield to violence, began to scream lustily from the window above; and luckily not in vain.

"It happened, that the family, who had gone on some expedition of pleasure in the morning, was just then returning; their road lay within a quarter of a mile of the turnpike; and in the silence of the night, the women's shrill voice reached their ears. They immediately desired the coachman to turn his horses heads in the direction the cries came from, and before the thieves had effected an entrance into the little fortification, they were scared by the sound of approaching wheels and took to flight."

"A dream of a very singular nature occurred to a young friend of mine," said Mr. S. "She was about fifteen at the time, and a schoolfellow who was going to be married had promised her that she should be one of the bridesmaids. The intended wedding was near at hand; insomuch that the dresses and everything was prepared-in short, the fixing of the day was only delayed by some small matter of business that was not completed. My young friend, to whom the whole thing was an exciting novelty, while impatiently waiting for the affair to come off, dreamt, one night, that a person in a very unusual costume, presented himself at her bedside and informed her that he was Brutus; and that he would reveal to her anything that she particularly desired to know; whereupon she begged him to tell when Miss L. would be married. Brutus answered 'Paulo post Græcas Kalendas.' When she awoke in the morning, she perfectly remembered the words; but not having the most distant idea of their meaning she ran to her brother to enquire if he could explain them. He told her that they were equivalent to *never*. The prophecy was fulfilled; obstacles entirely unforseen arose, and the couple were never united."

"Some years ago," said Dr. Forster, "two young friends of mine were staying at Naples, when one of them told the other that he had on the preceding night, seen in his sleep, the face of a beautiful woman; but the features were disfigured by a horrible expression-and that it was, somehow, impressed on his mind that he was in danger, and that he must be on his guard against her. The conviction was so strong as to create considerable uneasiness, and he never went out without scrutinizing every female face he saw; but some weeks past without any fulfilment of his dream or vision, and gradually the impression faded. However, he was one day on the Chiaja, surrounded by several people, who like himself, were observing a gang of convicts going to the Castle of St. Elmo; when something occasioned him suddenly to turn his head, and there, close behind him, he recognized the beautiful face of his dream. By an instinctive impulse, he sprang aside, and at the same moment felt himself wounded in the back. The woman was seized and did not attempt to deny the act, but alleged that she had mistaken the young Englishman for another person who had done her an irreparable injury, expressing great regret at having wounded an unoffending stranger, and also at having failed in the revenge she sought. He told me that the dream saved his life; for that, had he not sprung aside, the wound would in all probability have been mortal."

Fifth Evening

"I have but one experience to relate," said Miss D., the next speaker. "When I was a child, I and my elder sister slept in two beds, placed close beside each other. We were in the country, and one night my father, going to the door, perceived an unusual light in the sky, and learnt on inquiry that there was a great fire a mile or two off. He said he'd go to see it, and the night being fine, my mother accompanied him, having first seen us safe in bed. She locked the chamber door, and took the key, thinking that every body would be out looking at the fire, and we might take the opportunity of playing tricks, for we were quite young at the time-not more than six or seven years old.

"After they were gone, we lay chattering, as children do, about our own little concerns, when our voices were suddenly arrested by terror. At the foot of my bed I perceived a figure, apparently kneeling, for I saw only the head-but that I saw distinctly-it looked dark and sad, and the eyes were intently fixed on me. I crept into my sister's bed, and neither of us dared to look up again till my mother returned, and came to see if we were asleep. We had not closed our eyes, and we told her what we had seen, agreeing perfectly in our account of it. The room was searched, but nothing unusual found. The incident made a lasting impression on my sister and myself, and we both remember the face as if we had seen it but yesterday."

One of the ladies present mentioned a very similar circumstance occurring to herself, but as she was alone at the time, she had always endeavoured to believe it an illusion.

"The first part of the story I am going to relate to you," said Dr. S., "was told me by an eminent man in my own profession, who had every opportunity of testing the truth of it; the latter part I give you on my own word.

"Some years ago there was a house in the suburbs of Dublin that had remained a long time unoccupied, in consequence, it was said, of its evil reputation-the report was, that it was haunted. People who had taken it got rid of it as soon as they could, and those who lived in the neighbourhood affirmed that they saw lights moving about the interior, and, sometimes, a lady in white standing at the window with a child in her arms, when they knew there was no living creature, except rats and mice, within the walls. The wise and learned laughed at these rumours; but still the house remained empty, and was getting into a very dilapidated state.

"The former owner of the house was dead. He was a miser or a misanthrope, or both; at all events, for several years he had lived in it utterly alone, and scarcely ever seen by any body. It was rumoured that for a short time a young female had been occasionally observed by the neighbours, but she disappeared as suddenly as she had appeared, and nobody knew whence she came, nor whither she was gone. His life was a mystery, and whether merely on this account, or whether there were better grounds for it, there had certainly existed a prejudice against him. However, as I said, he had been dead some years, and the relative to whom the property had fallen on his decease was naturally very anxious to let the house, and offered it to any occupant at an extremely low rent.

"At length, a gentleman who wanted to establish a manufactory, seeing that it would answer his purpose-for the premises were extensive, and there was some garden ground behind-took it, and erected buildings on this waste ground for his workmen to inhabit. Between the new part and the old there was a long vestibule, or covered passage, by which they might pass from one to the other without exposing themselves to the weather. A large door, which was open by day and closed at night, divided this passage in two, and on one side there was a small room or office, where a clerk sat and kept the books and memoranda, of various sorts, incident to a considerable business.

"However, the thing was scarcely set going and established before it reached the ears of the master that the workmen objected to pass the night on the premises; the reason alleged being that they were disturbed and alarmed by various sounds, especially footsteps, and the banging of the heavy door in the vestibule which divided the sleeping places from the workrooms. At first, the objection being thought absurd, was not attended to; next, it was supposed to be a trick of some of the workmen to frighten the others; but when it became serious, and they began to act upon it, and steady, respectable men declared they heard these things, the master, still persuaded it was some practical jokers amongst them mystifying the more simple, took measures, first, to ascertain if such sounds as they described were audible; and next, to discover who made them. For this purpose he sat up himself, and his clerks sat up, and exactly as had been described, at one o'clock this clatter and banging of doors commenced-that is, there was the sound; for the doors remained immovable, and though they heard footsteps they could see nobody.

"'Still,' said the manufacturer, who was not willing to be made the victim of this mischievous conspiracy, 'we must discover who it is; and we shall, when they are more off their guard,' and for this purpose it was arranged that a relation of his own, a young man in whose discretion and courage he had great confidence should sleep in the office.

"Accordingly, a bed was prepared there; and he arranged himself for that night or as many future nights as it might be necessary; determined not to relinquish the investigation till he had unravelled the mystery.

"At dawn of day, the next morning, there was a violent knocking at the outer door; an early passenger had found this young man in the street, with nothing on but his night dress, and in a state of delirium. He was taken home and Dr. W. was sent for. The result was a brain fever; but when he recovered, he said that he had gone to bed and to sleep, that he was wakened by a loud noise, and that just as he was about to rise to ascertain the cause, his door opened, and the apparition of a female dressed in white entered, and approached his bed side. He remembered no more, but being seized with horror, supposed he had got out of the window into the street, where he was found.

"This was, certainly, very extraordinary and very serious; still the persuasion that it was some mystification prevailed; and Dr. W.'s offer to pass a night in the office himself, was gladly accepted. He had informed me of the young man's illness and the cause of it; and when I heard of his intention, I requested leave to bear him company.

"The noise had not been interrupted by the catastrophe that had occurred, and nobody had slept in the office during the young man's confinement. The bed had been removed, but we declined having it re-placed, for we wished our intention to remain a secret; besides, we preferred watching through the night. It was not till the workmen had all retired that we took up our position, accompanied by a sharp little terrier of mine, and each armed with a pistol. We took care to go over the house, to make sure that nobody was concealed in it; and we examined every door and window to ascertain that it was secure. We had provided ourselves with refreshments also, to sustain our courage; and we entered upon our vigil with great hopes of detecting the imposition.

"Dr. W. is a most enlightened and agreeable companion, and we soon fell into a lively discussion that carried us away so entirely, that, I believe, we had both ceased to think of the object of our watch, when we were recalled to it by the clock in the vestibule striking one; and the loud bang that immediately followed, accompanied by the barking of our little dog, who had been aroused from a tranquil sleep by the uproar. W. and I seized our pistols, and rushed into the passage, followed by the terrier. We saw nothing to account for the noise; but we distinctly heard receding footsteps, which we hastened to pursue, at the same time urging on the dog; but instead of running forward, he slunk behind, with his tail between his legs, and kept at our heels the whole way. On we went, distinctly hearing the footsteps preceding us along the vestibule, down some steps, and, finally, down some stairs that led to an unused cellar-in one corner of which lay a heap of rubbish. Here the sound ceased. We removed the rubbish, and under it lay some bones, which we recognised at once as parts of a human skeleton. On further examination, we ascertained that they were the remains of a female and a new-born infant.

"They were buried, and the men were no more disturbed with these mysterious noises. Who the woman was, was never ascertained; nor was any further light thrown upon these strange circumstances."

Some remarks on the terror displayed by animals, on these occasions, elicited a curious story from Mrs. L. "They not only seem to see sometimes," she said, "what we do not; but occasionally to be gifted with a singular foreknowledge.

"Many years ago," she continued, "I and my husband went to pay a visit in the north. I am very fond of animals, and my attention was soon attracted by a dog that was not particularly handsome, but seemed gifted with extraordinary intelligence.

"'I see,' said my hostess, 'you are struck with that dog. Well, he is the most mysterious creature; he not only opens and shuts the door, and rings the bell, and does all sorts of wonderful things, but I am sure he understands every word we say, and that he knows as well what I am saying now as you do. Moreover, we got him in a very unaccountable manner.

"'One night, not long ago, we had been out to dinner; and on returning at a pretty late hour, we found the gentleman stretched out comfortably on the dining-room rug. Where in the world did this dog come from? I said to the servants. They couldn't tell; they declared the doors had been long shut, and that they had never set eyes on him till that minute.'

"'Well,' I said, 'don't turn him out; he'll no doubt be claimed by some one in the neighbourhood-for he had quite the manners and air of a dog accustomed to good society; and I liked his large, expressive eyes. He made himself quite at home; and now we have discovered what a strangely intelligent creature he is, I hope no one will claim him, for I should be very sorry to part with him. But,' added she, 'poor Mrs. X. can't endure him.' Mrs. X., I must mention, was a widow lady, also on a visit there, with an only son.

"'Why?' said I.

"'It is rather singular, certainly,' said she; but whenever young X. is in the room, the dog never takes his eyes off his face-you see he has peculiar eyes-they're full of meaning; and out of doors he does the same.'

"'Perhaps the dog has taken a fancy to him?' I suggested.

"'It does not seem to be that; no, I think he likes me and Mrs. C. and my children a great deal better. I can't tell what it is; but if you watch, you'll see it.'

"I did, and it was really remarkable, and evidently annoyed Mrs. X. very much. The young man affected to laugh at it, but I don't think he liked it altogether.

"Suddenly, one evening, Mrs. X.—whose visit was to have extended to some weeks longer, announced that she should take her departure in a few days. I suspected this move was occasioned by her desire to get away from the dog, and so did my hostess-and we both thought it absurd.

"Mr. L. being obliged to return to London, we took our leave the morning after this announcement was made; but we had scarcely arrived there, when a letter from my friend followed, informing me that young Mr. X. had been unfortunately drowned in the fish-pond, and that the dog had never been seen since the accident, though they had made inquiries and sought for him in every direction. Whence he came, or whither he went, they were never able to discover.

"But," said Mrs. L., "as this is not a ghost story, I will tell you another anecdote that belongs more legitimately to the subjects you are treating of. Once, when we were travelling in the North, Mr. L. fell ill of a fever at Paisley. This detained us there, and the minister called on us. When Mr. L. recovered, we returned his visit; and, in the course of conversation, some of the old customs of the Scotch fell under discussion; amongst others the *cutty stool*, which we had heard still subsisted.

"'Why don't you abolish it?' said Mr. L. 'It would be much better to amend people by other influences than exposure.'

"'Well, sir,' said the good man, 'that was my opinion also; and I had determined to do it. Before taking the step, however, I thought it advisable to publish my reasons; and I was one day sitting at the table writing on the subject, when I looked up, and beheld my father, who was minister here before me, and died in this manse, sitting on the opposite side of the table.'

"'Don't do any such thing, David,' said he; 'morality is loose enough; don't make it looser.'"

Sixth Evening

"The most interesting circumstance of the ghostly kind that I know, as really authentic," said Madame S., "is what happened to the late Lord C., when he was a young man-it is an old story, and you must have heard of the *Radiant Boy*; but as I had it from a member of the family, perhaps you will accept it as my contribution.

"Captain S., who was afterwards Lord C., when he was a young man, happened to be quartered in Ireland. He was fond of sport; and one day the pursuit of game carried him so far that he lost his way. The weather, too, had become very rough, and in this strait he presented himself at the door of a gentleman's house, and sending in his card, requested shelter for the night. The hospitality of the Irish country gentry is proverbial; the master of the house received him warmly, said he feared he could not make him so comfortable as he could have wished, his house being full of visitors already-added to which, some strangers, driven by the inclemency of the night, had sought shelter before him, but that such accommodation as he could give he was heartily welcome to; whereupon he called his butler, and committing his guest to his good offices, told him he must put him up somewhere, and do the best he could for him. There was no lady, the gentleman being a widower.

"Captain S. found the house crammed, and a very jolly party it was. His host invited him to stay, and promised him good shooting if he would prolong his visit a few days; and, in fine, he thought himself extremely fortunate to have fallen into such pleasant quarters.

"At length, after an agreeable evening, they all retired to bed, and the butler conducted him to a large room, almost divested of furniture, but with a blazing peat fire in the grate, and a shake down on the floor, composed of cloaks and other heterogeneous materials.

"Nevertheless, to the tired limbs of Captain S., who had had a hard day's shooting, it looked very inviting; but before he lay down, he thought it advisable to take off some of the fire, which was blazing up the chimney, in what he thought, an alarming manner. Having done this, he stretched himself upon the couch, and soon fell asleep.

"He believed he had slept about a couple of hours when he awoke suddenly, and was startled by such a vivid light in the room, that he thought it was on fire, but on turning to look at the grate he saw the fire was out, though it was from the chimney the light proceeded. He sat up in bed, trying to discover what it was, when he perceived, gradually disclosing itself, the form of a beautiful naked boy, surrounded by a dazzling radiance. The boy looked at him earnestly, and then the vision faded, and all was dark. Captain S., so far from supposing what he had seen to be of a spiritual nature, had no doubt that the host, or the visitors, had been amusing themselves at his expense, and trying to frighten him. Accordingly he felt indignant at the liberty; and on the following morning, when he appeared at breakfast, he took care to evince his displeasure by the reserve of his demeanour, and by announcing his intention to depart immediately. The host expostulated, reminding him of his promise to stay and shoot. Captain S. coldly excused himself and, at length, the gentleman seeing something was wrong, took him aside, and pressed for an explanation; whereupon Captain S., without entering into particulars, said that he had been made the victim of a sort of practical joking that he thought quite unwarrantable with a stranger.

"The gentleman considered this not impossible amongst a parcel of thoughtless young men, and appealed to them to make an apology; but one and all, on honour, denied the impeachment. Suddenly, a thought seemed to strike him; he clapt his hand to his forehead, uttered an exclamation, and rang the bell.

"'Hamilton,' said he to the butler, 'where did Captain S. sleep last night?'

"'Well, Sir,' replied the man, in an apologetic tone,' 'you know every place was full-the gentlemen were lying on the floor, three or four in a room-so I gave him the *Boy's Room*; but I lit a blazing fire to keep him from coming out.'

"'You were very wrong,' said the host, 'you know I have positively forbidden you to put any one there, and have taken the furniture out of the room to ensure its not being occupied.' Then retiring with Captain S., he informed him very gravely of the nature of the phenomenon he had seen; and, at length, being pressed for further information, he confessed that there existed a tradition in his family, that whoever the *Radiant Boy* appeared to will rise to the summit of power; and when he had reached the climax, will die a violent death, and I must say, he added, that the records that have been kept of his appearance go to confirm this persuasion.

"I need not remind you," said Madam S., "what a remarkable confirmation was afforded by the life and death of Lord C."

"I had never heard these particulars before; but I had heard the story of Lord C.'s *Radiant Boy* alluded to, ápropos of the case of the Rev. Mr. A., who saw a very similar apparition some years ago at C. Castle. I have related this case in the 'Night Side of Nature.' I received the particulars from a relation of Mr. A.'s, who was himself surviving at the time I published it."

"It is curious," observed Mrs. E., "how many houses in the north of England where I have been lately residing have something of this sort attached to them. Some friends of mine not long ago heard of a very pretty place to let, and finding the rent unusually moderate they took it. They were delighted with their new residence; and often wondered that the proprietor, with whom they were slightly acquainted, did not either live there himself, or insist on more money for it.

"After they had been there some time, his brother, that is, the brother of the proprietor, who did not live very far off, called one morning to see them; and asked them how they liked the place. They expressed their extreme satisfaction; adding, 'We wonder your brother does not live here himself.'

"'There are reasons why it does not suit our family,' he answered.

"When he was going away, my friends proposed to walk through the grounds with him; they had to cross a little brook not far from the house; and as they did so, a hare sprang past them and they all stopt and turned round to look at her, by which means they had a full view of the house.

"'Good Heavens!' exclaimed the visitor, 'there she is!'

"'Where?' enquired my friend, thinking he alluded to the hare.

"'Is any of your family ill?' asked the stranger.

"'No they answered;' and following the direction of his eyes, they observed at one of the upper windows of the house, a female figure in white, and enveloped in what looked like grave clothes.

"The visitor appearing much agitated, my friend rushed back and ran up to the floor where the female had appeared; and not only was there no one there, but he found that the window was that of a vestibule and much too high from the ground for any one to reach.

"On returning to their visitor, he said 'one of us will die before this year has expired; it is an unfailing omen in our family, and caused us so much distress, that that is the real reason why we do not live here. But it concerns nobody but ourselves; you will never be troubled by her visitations.' The destiny fell on the seer himself this time; he was dead before the year had expired.

"There is another house in the same part of the county, where sometime ago a young friend of mine, one of three sisters, went on a visit for a short time. The first night, after she got into bed, she was startled by the most terrific screams she ever heard, which appeared close to her door. She jumped up and opened it, but there was nobody there. The next day she mentioned the circumstance, but the old lady she was visiting, said her ears must have deceived her, and turned the conversation; but she heard it again several times, and was quite sure there was no mistake. When she went home she told her sisters, who laughed at her; but each of them went to visit subsequently at the same house and heard precisely the same thing; but as it was evidently an unpleasant subject to their hostess, they could get no information on the subject."

"A near relation of mine," said Lord N., "is living in a place at present, where there is very much the same annoyance, and three families successively, had left the house in consequence of it. The building is large, part of it very old, and it is surrounded by a fine park; nevertheless, it has been found difficult to get a tenant-or, at least, to keep one. My relation was warned of the inconvenience before he took it. It is said that a lady was murdered there by her husband; at all events, there is one room-one of the best in the house, shut up, and never allowed to be opened. Whoever sleeps in the room under this, is liable to be disturbed by extraordinary noises-footsteps and moving of furniture, &c.; but the most strange thing is, that every now and then a dreadful piercing scream is heard through the house, that brings any strangers who happen to be there, out of their rooms, in terror, to enquire what has occurred. The family who resided there before, met the apparition of a lady occasionally, and left the place in consequence. My relations have never seen anything; but everybody who stays there any time hears the screams.

"Another relation of mine, a very religious person, and as she belongs to the free church of Scotland, most opposed to the belief in ghosts, went some time since to pay a visit at an old place belonging to our family. On the morning after her arrival, she announced at breakfast that she was going away. She gave no reason, but went, to the consternation of her host. With much difficulty, he has since extracted from her, that in the night an apparition appeared at the foot of her bed —a man dressed in an old-fashioned brown suit. He spoke to her, and some conversation passed-the subject of which she declares she will never disclose; she says it was not a good spirit, and nothing would induce her to visit the place again. This house has always been said to be haunted, but this is the only instance I know of the family themselves seeing anything of the sort; but no better evidence could be adduced of such a phenomenon than that of the lady in question. Nobody ever doubted her word, and a more confirmed disbeliever in ghosts never existed.

"A rather curious thing happened to myself lately," continued Lord N. "I went to visit some friends at the Lakes. As they had no vacant rooms, I engaged apartments near them for myself and servant. The house was small, quite modern, and as un-ghostly as possible. I always dined with my friends, and went to my lodgings about twelve o'clock, and I had been there five or six nights without anything unusual occurring. On the fourth or fifth evening, I had returned home rather earlier than usual, and instead of going to bed, I sat down to write a letter. While so engaged, I heard what I thought was a boy cracking a whip close to the drawing-room door. I paid no attention to it at first, though rather wondering at the hour chosen for the amusement. However, as it continued unintermittingly, and grew louder, I got up and opened the door, with the intention of desiring the child to go away. There was no one there. It then occurred to me that my ears must have deceived me, and that the sound might have proceeded from some explosive substance in my bedroom fire. The room was on the same floor, and the door shut; but when I opened it, I found the fire almost out-certainly not in a state to produce the noises I had heard. I went forward to stir it, and while doing so, the whip was cracked over my shoulder. I turned round quickly, but could see nothing, and I returned to the drawing-room, and had just seated myself again, when I was amazed to see the table rise about a foot perpendicularly into the air, and at the same moment, both the candles that were on it went out, without being upset or even moved. There was a fire, so that I was not quite in the dark, and I re-lighted them; after which the whip began cracking again vigorously, and cracked on till I went to bed and afterwards. I stayed in these apartments a fortnight or three weeks longer; and once, again, I heard the whip, but much fainter and for a shorter time; and one night there were distinct rappings on the mantel-piece, and afterwards on the dressing-table.

"I could make no discovery in regard to these phenomena; and I leave it to the company to decide whether they were of a spiritual nature or not. The only other thing of the sort that ever happened to me was this: —I was travelling on the Continent, and not being very well, was lying in bed, when I suddenly saw the door open, and two of my brothers walk through the room, dressed in deep mourning. I rang the bell furiously, and the people came, but could in no way explain what had happened. I shortly received letters, announcing that another brother had died at that time.

"I will mention another instance that occurred in our family a few years since. During my grandfather's last illness, all the family were assembled at K. Castle, except my brother John, with whom he was not on good terms. While we were living there, waiting to see what turn the illness would take, John died very unexpectedly, but we resolved not to mention the circumstance to Lord A., as it might affect him injuriously; it was therefore kept a profound secret.

"One day, some little time afterwards, Lord A. had been asleep in his arm-chair, and on waking, he suddenly exclaimed, 'I shall see John on Thursday!' This was on a Monday, and he died on the Thursday following."

"A relation of mine," said Mrs. L., "had a friend with whom a great intimacy had subsisted for many years, but a subject of difference arose that embittered her feelings towards this lady to such a degree, that she felt reconciliation impossible. They continued to live in the same town, but all intercourse was at an end.

"One morning, lately, she was lying awake in her bed, when the door opened, and this lady came in; approaching the bed side, she spoke in a friendly manner, and entered into explanations with regard to the misunderstanding. My relation was not frightened during this interview; but when it was over, and she was gone, she suspected the nature of the visit. When her maid came to her room, she enquired if there had been any news of Miss ——. The servant answered, none; but presently afterwards, a person called to mention the lady's death, which had taken place that morning."

"For my part," said Sir A. C., "I am acquainted with a circumstance that has settled entirely any doubts I might have entertained on the subject of ghosts. Not many miles from my place in S—shire, there is a seat belonging to some connexions of my own. At the time I am about to refer to, an old lady was in possession, and it so happened, that a matter of business arose regarding the heirs of the property, which made it necessary to refer to the title deeds. To the surprise and dismay of the family they could not be found. A vigorous search was instituted, in vain; and the circumstance so preyed on my old relation's mind that she at length committed suicide, under the impression that some one else would lay claim to the estate.

"After her death people complained that they could not live there-the place they said was haunted by this old lady, who, with her grey hair dishevelled, and dressed exactly as she used to be in her life time, they described as walking about the house, looking into drawers and cupboards, and incessantly searching for her deeds. We, of course, did not believe in the story, and were not even altogether convinced when the house, after being let to several strangers in succession, who all gave it up on the same plea, seemed destined to remain without an inhabitant.

"It had stood empty two or three years, though offered at a very low rent, when a lady and gentleman from the West Indies came into the neighbourhood to visit some acquaintance, and being in want of a residence, and hearing this was to be had on very reasonable terms, they proposed to take it. Their friends told them of the objection made by preceding tenants, but they laughed with scorn at the idea of losing so good a house on account of a ghost; so they closed the bargain, took possession of the place, and sent for their family to join them.

"The children, the youngest of whom was between three and four, and the eldest about ten, were, as a temporary arrangement, placed on the first night of their arrival to sleep in one room; but the next morning, when their mother went at a very early hour to see how they were, to her surprise, she found them all wide awake. They were looking pale and weary, and began with one voice to complain that they had been kept awake all night by such a disagreeable old lady, who would keep coming into the room, and looking for something in the drawers. 'I told her I wished she'd go away,' said the eldest, 'and then she did go; but she came back; and we don't like her. Who is she, mamma? Is she to live with us?'

"They then, on being questioned, described her appearance, which exactly coincided with the account given by the former tenants. I can vouch for the truth of these circumstances; and since these children had, certainly, never heard a word on the subject of the apparition, and had, indeed, no idea that it was one, 'I think the evidence,' said Sir A. C., 'is quite unexceptionable.'

"I should say so, too, if it referred to any other question," said Mr. E., a barrister, who happened to be present when the story was related; "but on the subject of ghosts I cannot think any evidence sufficient."

"A state of mind by no means uncommon," I said, "and which it is, of course, in vain to contend with. I can only wonder and admire the confidence that can venture to prejudge so interesting and important a subject of inquiry."

Seventh Evening

“My story will be a very short one,” said Mrs. M.; ”for I must tell you that though, like every body else, I have heard a great many ghost stories, and have met people who assured me they had seen such things, I cannot, for my own part, bring myself to believe in them; but a circumstance occurred when I was abroad, that you may perhaps consider of a ghostly nature, though I cannot.

”I was travelling through Germany, with no one but my maid-it was before the time of railways, and on my road from Leipsic to Dresden, I stopt at an inn that appeared to have been long ago part of an aristocratic residence —a castle in short; for there was a stone wall and battlements, and a tower at one side; while the other was a prosaic-looking, square building that had evidently been added in modern times. The inn stood at one end of a small village, in which some of the houses looked so antique that they might, I thought, be coeval with the castle itself. There were a good many travellers, but the host said he could accommodate me; and when I asked to see my room, he led me up to the towers, and showed me a tolerably comfortable one. There were only two apartments on each floor; so I asked him if I could have the other for my maid, and he said yes, if no other traveller arrived. None came, and she slept there.

”I supped at the table d'hôte, and retired to bed early, as I had an excursion to make on the following day; and I was sufficiently tired with my journey to fall asleep directly.

”I don’t know how long I had slept-but I think some hours, when I awoke quite suddenly, almost with a start, and beheld near the foot of the bed, the most hideous, dreadful-looking old woman, in an antique dress, that imagination can conceive. She seemed to be approaching me-not as if walking, but gliding, with her left arm and hand extended towards me.

“ ‘Merciful God deliver me!’ I exclaimed under my first impulse of amazement; and as I said the words she disappeared.”

“Then, though you don’t believe in ghosts, you thought it was one when you saw it,” said I.

”I don’t know what I thought —I admit I was a good deal frightened, and it was a long time before I fell asleep again.

“In the morning,” continued Mrs. M., ”my maid knocked, and I told her to come in; but the door was locked, and I had to get out of bed to admit her —I thought I might have forgotten to fasten it. As soon as I was up, I examined every part of the room, but I could find nothing to account for this intrusion. There was neither trap or moving panell, or door that I could see, except the one I had locked. However, I made up my mind not to speak of the circumstance, for I fancied I must have been deceived in supposing myself awake, and that it was only a dream; more particularly as there was no light in my room, and I could not comprehend how I could have seen this woman.

”I went out early, and was away the greater part of the day. When I returned I found more travellers had arrived, and that they had given the room next mine to a German lady and her daughter, who were at the table d'hôte. I therefore had a bed made up in my room for my maid; and before I lay down, I searched thoroughly, that I might be sure nobody was concealed there.

”In the middle of the night —I suppose about the same time I had been disturbed on the preceding one —I and my maid were awakened by a piercing scream; and I heard the voice of the German girl in the adjoining room, exclaiming, ‘Ach! meine mutter! meine mutter!’

“For some time afterwards I heard them talking, and then I fell asleep-wondering, I confess, whether they had had a visit from the frightful old woman. They left me in no doubt the next morning. They came down to breakfast greatly excited-told everybody the cause-described the old woman exactly as I had seen her, and departed from the house incontinently, declaring they would not stay there another hour.”

“What did the host say to it?” we asked.

“Nothing; he said we must have dreamed it-and I suppose we did.”

“Your story,” said I, ”reminds me of a very interesting letter which I received soon after the publication of ‘The Night side of Nature.’ It was from a clergyman who gave his name, and said he was chaplain to a nobleman. He related that in a house he inhabited, or had inhabited, a lady had one evening gone up stairs, and seen, to her amazement, in a room, the door of which was open, a lady in an antique dress, standing before a chest of drawers, and apparently examining their contents. She stood still, wondering who this stranger could be, when the figure turned her face towards her, and, to her horror, she saw there were no eyes. Other members of the family saw the same apparition also. I believe there were further particulars; but I unfortunately lost this letter, with some others, in the confusion of changing my residence.

"The absence of eyes I take to be emblematical of moral blindness; for in the world of spirits there is no deceiving each other by false seemings; as we are, so we appear."

"Then," said Mrs. W. C., "the apparition-if it was an apparition-that two of my servants saw lately, must be in a very degraded state.

"There is a road, and on one side of it a path, just beyond my garden wall. Not long ago two of my servants were in the dusk of the evening walking up this path, when they saw a large, dark object coming towards them. At first, they thought it was an animal; and when it got close, one of them stretched out her hand to touch it; but she could feel nothing, and it passed on between her and the garden wall, although there was *no space*, the path being only wide enough for two; and on looking back, they saw it walking down the hill behind them. Three men were coming up on the path; and as the thing approached, they jumped off into the road.

"'Good heavens, what is that!' cried the women.

"'I don't know,' replied the men; 'I never saw such a thing as that before.'

"The women came home greatly agitated; and we have since heard there is a tradition that the spot is haunted by the ghost of a man who was killed in a quarry close by."

"I have travelled a great deal," said our next speaker, the Chevalier de La C. G.; and, certainly, I have never been in any country where instances of these spiritual appearances were not adduced on apparently credible authority. I have heard numerous stories of the sort, but the one that most readily occurs to me at present, was told to me not long ago, in Paris, by Count P. —the nephew of the celebrated Count P. whose name occurs in the history of the remarkable incidents connected with the death of the Emperor Paul.

"Count P., my authority for the following story, was attached to the Russian embassy; and he told me, one evening, when the conversation turned on the inconveniences of travelling in the East of Europe, that, on one occasion, when in Poland, he found himself about seven o'clock in an autumn evening on a forest road, where there was no possibility of finding a house of public entertainment within many miles. There was a frightful storm; the road, not good at the best, was almost impracticable from the weather, and his horses were completely knocked up. On consulting his people what was best to be done, they said, that to go back was as impossible as to go forward; but that by turning a little out of the main road, they should soon reach a castle where possibly shelter might be procured for the night. The count gladly consented, and it was not long before they found themselves at the gate of what appeared a building on a very splendid scale. The courier quickly alighted and rang at the bell, and while waiting for admission, he enquired who the castle belonged to, and was told that it was Count X's.

"It was some time before the bell was answered, but at length an elderly man appeared at a wicket, with a lantern, and peeped out. On perceiving the equipage, he came forward and stept up to the carriage, holding the light aloft to discover who was inside. Count P. handed him his card, and explained his distress.

"'There is no one here, my lord,' replied the man, 'but myself and my family; the castle is not inhabited.'

"'That's bad news,' said the count; 'but nevertheless, you can give me what I am most in need of, and that is-shelter for the night.'

"'Willingly,' said the man, 'if your lordship will put up with such accommodation as we can hastily prepare.'

"'So,' said the count, 'I alighted and walked in; and the old man unbarred the great gates to admit my carriages and people. We found ourselves in an immense *couer*, with the castle *en face*, and stables and offices on each side. As we had a *fourgon* with us, with provender for the cattle and provisions for ourselves, we wanted nothing but beds and a good fire; and as the only one lighted was in the old man's apartments, he first took us there. They consisted of a *suite* of small rooms in the left wing, that had probably been formerly occupied by the upper servants. They were comfortably furnished, and he and his large family appeared to be very well lodged. Besides the wife, there were three sons, with their wives and children, and two nieces; and in a part of the offices, where I saw a light, I was told there were labourers and women servants, for it was a valuable estate, with a fine forest, and the sons acted as *gardes chasse*.

"'Is there much game in the forest?' I asked.

"'A great deal of all sorts,' they answered.

"'Then I suppose during the season the family live here?'

"'Never,' they replied. 'None of the family ever reside here.'

"'Indeed!' I said; how is that? It seems a very fine place.'

"'Superb,' answered the wife of the custodian; 'but the castle is haunted.'

"She said this with a simple gravity that made me laugh; upon which they all stared at me with the most edifying amazement.

"'I beg your pardon,' I said; 'but you know, perhaps, in great cities, such as I usually inhabit, there are no ghosts.'

"'Indeed!' said they. 'No ghosts!'

"'At least,' I said, 'I never heard of any; and we don't believe in such things.'

"They looked at each other with surprise, but said nothing; not appearing to have any desire to convince me. 'But do you mean to say,' said I, 'that that is the reason the family don't live here, and that the castle is abandoned on that account?'

"'Yes,' they replied, 'that is the reason nobody has resided here for many years.'

"'But how can you live here then?'

"'We are never troubled in this part of the building,' said she. 'We hear noises, but we are used to that.'

"'Well, if there is a ghost, I hope I shall see it,' said I.

"'God forbid!' said the woman, crossing herself. 'But we shall guard against that; your seigneurie will sleep not far from this, where you will be quite safe.'

"'Oh! but,' said I, 'I am quite serious, if there is a ghost, I should particularly like to see him, and I should be much obliged to you to put me in the apartments he most frequents.'

"They opposed this proposition earnestly, and begged me not to think of if; besides, they said if any thing was to happen to my lord, how should they answer for it; but as I insisted, the women went to call the members of the family who were lighting fires and preparing beds in some rooms on the same floor as they occupied themselves. When they came they were as earnest against the indulgence of my wishes as the women had been. Still I insisted.

"'Are you afraid,' I said, 'to go yourselves in the haunted chambers?'

"'No,' they answered. 'We are the custodians of the castle and have to keep the rooms clean and well aired lest the furniture be spoiled-my lord talks always of removing it, but it has never been removed yet-but we would not sleep up there for all the world.'

"'Then it is the upper floors that are haunted?'

"'Yes, especially the long room, no one could pass a night there; the last that did is in a lunatic asylum now at Warsaw,' said the custodian.

"'What happened to him?'

"'I don't know,' said the man; 'he was never able to tell.'

"'Who was he?' I asked.

"'He was a lawyer. My lord did business with him; and one day he was speaking of this place, and saying that it was a pity he was not at liberty to pull it down and sell the materials; but he cannot, because it is family property and goes with the title; and the lawyer said he wished it was his, and that no ghost should keep him out of it. My lord said that it was easy for any one to say that who knew nothing about it, and that he must suppose the family had not abandoned such a fine place without good reasons. But the lawyer said it was some trick, and that it was coiners, or robbers, who had got a footing in the castle, and contrived to frighten people away that they might keep it to themselves; so my lord said if he could prove that he should be very much obliged to him, and more than that, he would give him a great sum —I don't know how much. So the lawyer said, he would; and my lord wrote to me that he was coming to inspect the property, and I was to let him do any thing he liked.

"'Well, he came, and with him his son, a fine young man and a soldier. They asked me all sorts of questions, and went over the castle and examined every part of it. From what they said, I could see that they thought the ghost was all nonsense, and that I and my family were in collusion with the robbers or coiners. However, I did not care for that, my lord knew that the castle had been haunted before I was born.

"'I had prepared rooms on this floor for them-the same I am preparing for your lordship, and they slept there, keeping the keys of the upper rooms to themselves, so I did not interfere with them. But one morning, very early, we were awakened by some one knocking at our bedroom door, and when we opened it, we saw Mr. Thaddeus-that was the lawyer's son-standing there half-drest and as pale as a ghost; and he said his father was very ill and he begged us to go to him; to our surprise he led us up stairs to the haunted chamber, and there we found the poor gentleman speechless, and we thought they had gone up there early and that he had had a stroke. But it was not so; Mr. Thaddeus said, that after we were all in bed, they had gone up there to pass the night. I know they thought that there was no ghost but us, and that's why they would not let us know their intention. They laid down upon some sofas, wrapt up in their fur cloaks, and resolved to keep awake, and they did so for some time, but at last the young man was overcome by drowsiness, he struggled against it, but could not conquer it, and the last thing he recollects was his father shaking him and saying 'Thaddeus, Thaddeus, for God's sake keep awake!' But he could not, and he knew no more till he woke and saw that day was breaking, and found his father sitting in a corner of the room speechless, and looking like a corpse; and there he was when we went up. The young man thought he'd been taken ill or had a stroke, as we supposed at first; but when we found they had passed the night in the haunted chambers, we had no doubt what had happened-he had seen some terrible sight and so lost his senses.'

"'He lost his senses, I should say, from terror when his son fell asleep,' said I, 'and he felt himself alone. He could have been a man of no nerve. At all events, what you tell me raises my curiosity. Will you take me up stairs and shew me those rooms?'

"'Willingly,' said the man, and fetching a bunch of keys and a light, and calling one of his sons to follow him with another, he led the way up the great staircase to a suite of apartments on the first floor. The rooms were lofty and large, and the man said the furniture was very handsome, but old. Being all covered with canvas cases, I could not judge of it. 'Which is the long room?' I said.

"Upon which he led me into a long narrow room that might rather have been called a gallery. There were sofas along each side, something like a dais at the upper end; and several large pictures hanging on the walls.

"I had with me a bull dog, of a very fine breed, that had been given me in England by Lord F. She had followed me up stairs-indeed, she followed me every where-and I watched her narrowly as she went smelling about, but there were no indications of her perceiving any thing extraordinary. Beyond this gallery there was only a small octagon room, with a door that led out upon another staircase. When I had examined it all thoroughly, I returned to the long room and told the man, as that was the place especially frequented by the ghost, I should feel much obliged if he would allow me to pass the night there. I could take upon myself to say that Count X., would have no objection.

"'It is not that,' replied the man; 'but the danger to your lordship,' and he conjured me not to insist on such a perilous experiment.

"When he found I was resolved, he gave way, but on condition that I signed a paper, stating that in spite of his representations I had determined to sleep in the long room.

"I confess, the more anxious these people seemed to prevent my sleeping there, the more curious I was; not that I believed in the ghost the least in the world. I thought that the lawyer had been right in his conjecture, but that he hadn't nerve enough to investigate whatever he saw or heard; and that they had succeeded in frightening him out of his senses. I saw what an excellent place these people had got, and how much it was their interest to maintain the idea that the castle was uninhabitable. Now, I have pretty good nerves —I have been in situations that have tried them severely-and I did not believe that any ghost, if there was such a thing, or any jugglery by which a semblance of one might be contrived, would shake them. As for any real danger, I did not apprehend it; the people knew who I was, and any mischief happening to me would have led to consequences they well understood. So they lighted fires in both the grates of the gallery, and as they had abundance of dry wood, they soon blazed up. I was determined not to leave the room after I was once in it, lest, if my suspicions were correct, they might have time to make their arrangements; so I desired my people to bring up my supper, and I ate it there.

"My courier said he had always heard the castle was haunted, but he dare say there was no ghost but the people below, who had a very comfortable berth of it; and he offered to pass the night with me, but I declined any companion and preferred trusting to myself and my dog. My valet, on the contrary, strongly advised me against the enterprize, assuring me that he had lived with a family in France whose château was haunted, and had left his place in consequence.

"By the time I had finished my supper it was ten o'clock, and every thing was prepared for the night. My bed, though an impromptu, was very comfortable, made of amply stuffed cushions and thick coverlets, placed in front of the fire. I was provided with light and plenty of wood; and I had my regimental cutlass, and a case of excellent pistols, which I carefully primed and loaded in presence of the custodian, saying, you see I am determined to fire at the ghost, so if he cannot stand a bullet, he had better not pay me a visit.

"The old man shook his head calmly, but made no answer. Having desired the courier, who said he should not go to bed, to come up stairs immediately if he heard the report of fire-arms, I dismissed my people and locked the doors, barricading each with a heavy ottoman besides. There was no arras or hangings of any sort behind which a door could be concealed; and I went round the room, the walls of which were pannelled with white and gold, knocking every part, but neither the sound, nor Dido, the dog, gave any indications of there being anything unusual. Then I undressed and lay down with my sword and my pistols beside me; and Dido at the foot of my bed, where she always slept.

"I confess I was in a state of pleasing excitement; my curiosity and my love of adventure were roused; and whether it was ghost, or robber, or coiner, I was to have a visit from, the interview was likely to be equally interesting. It was half-past ten when I lay down; my expectations were too vivid to admit of sleep; and after an attempt at a French novel, I was obliged to give it up; I could not fix my attention to it. Besides, my chief care was not to be surprised. I could not help thinking the custodian and his family had some secret way of getting into the room, and I hoped to detect them in the fact; so I lay with my eyes and ears open in a position that gave me a view of every part of it, till my travelling clock struck twelve, which being pre-eminently the ghostly hour, I thought the critical moment was arrived. But no, no sound, no interruption of any sort to the silence and solitude of the night occurred. When half-past twelve, and one struck, I pretty well made up my mind that I should be disappointed in my expectations, and that the ghost, whoever he was, knew better than to encounter Dido and a brace of well charged pistols; but just as I arrived at this conclusion, an unaccountable *frisson* came over me, and I saw Dido, who tired with her day's journey, had lain till now quietly curled up asleep, begin to move, and slowly get upon her feet. I thought she was only going to turn, but, instead of lying down, she stood still with her ears erect and her head towards the dais, uttering a low growl.

"The dais, I should mention, was but the skeleton of a dais, for the draperies were taken off. There was only remaining a canopy covered with crimson velvet, and an arm chair covered with velvet too, but cased in canvas like the rest of the furniture. I had examined this part of the room thoroughly, and had moved the chair aside to ascertain that there was nothing under it.

"Well, I sat up in bed and looked steadily in the same direction as the dog, but I could see nothing at first, though it appeared that she did; but as I looked, I began to perceive something like a cloud in the chair, while at the same time a chill which seemed to pervade the very marrow in my bones crept through me, yet the fire was good; and it was not the chill of fear, for I cocked my pistols with perfect self possession and abstained from giving Dido the signal to advance, because I wished eagerly to see the denouement of the adventure.

"Gradually, this cloud took a form, and assumed the shape of a tall white figure that reached from the ceiling to the floor of the dais, which was raised by two steps. At him, Dido! At him! I said, and away she dashed to the steps, but instantly turned and crept back completely cowed. As her courage was undoubted, I own this astonished me, and I should have fired, but that I was perfectly satisfied that what I saw was not a substantial human form, for I had seen it grow into its present shape and height from the undefined cloud that first appeared in the chair. I laid my hand on the dog who had crept up to my side, and I felt her shaking in her skin. I was about to rise myself and approach the figure, though I confess I was a good deal awe struck, when it stepped majestically from the dais, and seemed to be advancing. 'At him!' I said, 'At him, Dido!' and I gave the dog every encouragement to go forward; she made a sorry attempt, but returned when she had got half way and crouched beside me whining with terror. The figure advanced upon me; the cold became icy; the dog crouched and trembled; and I, as it approached, honestly confess, said Count P., that I hid my head under the bed clothes and did not venture to look up till morning. I know not what it was-as it passed over me I felt a sensation of undefinable horror, that no words can describe-and I can only say that nothing on earth would tempt me to pass another night in that room, and I am sure if Dido could speak, you'd find her of the same opinion.

"I had desired to be called at seven o'clock, and when the custodian, who accompanied my valet, found me safe and in my perfect senses, I must say the poor man appeared greatly relieved; and when I descended the whole family seemed to look upon me as a hero. I thought it only just to them to admit that something had happened in the night that I felt impossible to account for, and that I should not recommend any body who was not very sure of their nerves to repeat the experiment."

When the Chevalier had concluded this extraordinary story, I suggested that the apparition of the castle very much resembled that mentioned by the late professor Gregory, in his letters on mesmerism, as having appeared in the Tower of London some years ago, and from the alarm it created, having occasioned the death of a lady, the wife of an officer quartered there, and one of the sentries. Every one who had read that very interesting publication was struck by the resemblance.

Eighth Evening

"As this was our last evening, I was called upon for a story; but I pleaded that I had told all mine in the 'Night Side of Nature,' and of personal experience I had very little to tell; but I said I will give you the history of a visit I made several years ago to a haunted house although it resulted in almost nothing.

"After the publication of the 'Night Side,' I received many valuable communications—I wish I had kept a note of them all, but I never expected to publish again on the same subject. Amongst others, I received a letter from a gentleman called Mc. N., and as it contained several interesting particulars, I requested him to call on me. I remember, in the letter, he told me that a few years previously, he had been on an excursion from home, and that while stopping at an inn, one morning, about five o'clock, the door opened and his father entered; he came to the bedside, looked at him, and then went out again. The young man sprang from his bed, and followed him down stairs, where he lost sight of him. He returned home, and found his father had died on that morning.

"He was in a lawyer's office, and, amongst other things, he mentioned to me that there was not very far off a house said to be haunted, of which they had the charge, but that it was impossible to do anything with it. 'We offer it at a mere nominal rent, but no one will stay there.'

"I was often absent from home at this time, but for the next two or three years I sometimes met him and inquired about the house. The report was always the same; till, at length, no one would go into it; it was shut up-the shutters were closed, and the boys of the neighbourhood threw stones at the windows and broke the glass. Yet it was situated in a street where every other house was inhabited, and which had not been built many years.

"It was as much as six or seven years after I had first heard of this house, that I happened to mention the circumstance to some gentlemen of my acquaintance-very eminent men, with honest, inquiring minds; truth seekers, who, if she were in the bottom of a well, would have thought it right to go after her. As they had humility enough to feel that they could not pronounce upon a question that they had never studied or investigated, they expressed a wish to visit the house. Accordingly, I applied to Mr. Mc. N., who had the keys in his office, and he obligingly consented to accompany us. Our expedition was to be kept a profound secret; and it was so, till some time afterwards, when, like most other secrets, it got wind and it spread abroad.

"We started in a carriage, between eleven and twelve o'clock at night, taking with us a young girl who was easily mesmerised, and when in that state a good clairvoyante. She was not told the object of our journey, and had no means whatever of learning it. We said we were going to look at a house, and that that was the most convenient time for the gentleman to show it us. We did not drive to the door, but Mr. Mc. N. met us in the next street, where we alighted, lest we should attract observation. We walked to our destination, and Mr. Mc. N. explained to the policeman on duty who he was and where we were going, lest he should suspect mischief, and interrupt us. He then unlocked the door with the aid of the policeman's lantern, for it was a dark winter's night; and on entering, we found ourselves in a narrow passage.

"It was a small house, in no respect different from the others in the street. They seemed all of the same description. A narrow frontage, with one window and the door, on the ground floor; two windows above; two rooms on a floor, three stories in height, and a kitchen, scullery, and cellars underground.

"As soon as the door closed on us, we were in utter darkness, but we had provided ourselves with candles and matches, and when we had lighted them, we entered the back parlour, which Mr. Mc. N. had heard from the different inhabitants was the room in which they had met with most annoyance.

"The clairvoyante was then put to sleep, and asked if she liked the house, and would recommend us to take it. She shuddered and said 'No; that two people had been murdered there, and we should be *troubled*.' We asked in which room; she answered, 'it was before this house was built-that another house stood there then—a very old house.' This was not exactly on the same ground, but the room we were in was on part of it. She said that it was these murdered people who would trouble us. We asked if she could see them, and she answered 'no.'

"We then waited in silence to see if anything occurred; but nothing did, except a metallic sound at the door, which was ajar, like the striking of two pieces of iron. We all heard it, but could not say what occasioned it.

"After a little time, some one suggested that we should extinguish the lights. We did so, and were then in absolute darkness. There was but one window in the room, and that was coated with dust, and the shutter was shut; besides, as I have said, it was a very dark night, and this room, being at the back, looked into a yard, I believe; at all events, not into a street.

"Presently, the clairvoyante started, and exclaimed, 'Look there!' We saw nothing, and asked what it was.

"'There!' she said. 'There again! don't you see it?'

"'What?' we asked. 'The lights!' she said. 'There! Now!' These exclamations were made at intervals of two or three seconds.

"We all said we saw nothing whatever.

"'If Mrs. Crowe would take hold of my hand, I think she would see them,' she suggested.

"I did so; and then at intervals of a few seconds, I saw thrown up, apparently from the floor, waves of white light, faint, but perfectly distinct and visible. In order that I might know whether our perceptions of this phenomenon were simultaneous, I desired her, without speaking, to press my hand each time she saw it, which she did; and each time I distinctly saw the wave of white light. I saw it, at these intervals, as long as I held her hand and we were in the dark. Nobody saw it but she and myself; and we did not follow up the experiment by the others taking her hand, which we should have done.

"During this interval, another light suddenly appeared in the middle of the room, away from where we were standing, I saw a bright diamond of light, like an extremely vivid spark-only not the colour of fire; it was white, brilliant, and quiescent, but shed no rays. I did not mention this, because I wished to learn if it was visible to any body else-but nobody spoke of it; not even the clairvoyante. Whether she saw it or not, I cannot say. When the candles were re-lighted these lights were no longer visible. I and one of the gentlemen went over the house above and below, but saw nothing but the dust and desolation of a long uninhabited dwelling.

"When we came away, and Mr. Mc. N. had locked the door, we walked to the carriage. I said, 'then you none of you saw the waves of light.'

"'No,' said they.

"'Well,' said I, 'I certainly did, and I never saw anything like it before. Moreover, I saw another sort of light.'

"'Did you,' said Mr. Mc. N., interrupting me; 'was it a bright spark of light like the oxy-hydrogen light.'

"'Exactly,' said I. 'I could not think what to compare it to; but that was it.'

"I thus was certain that he had seen the same thing as myself; he had not spoken of it from a similar motive; he waited to have his impression confirmed by further testimony.

"You see our results were not great, but the visit was not wholly barren to me. Of course, many wise people will say, I did not see the lights, but that they were the offspring of my excited imagination. But I beg to say that my imagination was by no means excited. If I had been there *alone*, it would have been a different affair; for though I never saw a ghost nor ever fancied I did, I am afraid I should have been very nervous. But I was in exceedingly good company, with two very clever men, besides the lawyer, a lady, and the clairvoyante; so that my nerves were perfectly composed, as I should not object to seeing any ghost in such agreeable society. Moreover, I did not *expect* any result; because, there is very seldom any on these occasions, as ghosts appear we know not why; but certainly not because people wish to see them. They generally come when least expected and least thought of.

"Mr. Mc. N., on inquiry, learnt that unaccountable lights were amongst the things complained of. What occasioned them and the other phenomena, it had certainly been the proprietor's interest for many years to discover; it had also been the interest of numerous tenants, who having taken the house for a term, found themselves obliged to leave it at a sacrifice. Yet, for all those years, no explanation could be found for the annonyances but that the house was haunted. No tradition seems extant to account for its evil reputation. If what the clairvoyante said was true, the murders must have occurred long ago.

"A gentleman, an inhabitant of the same city, once mentioned to me that a friend of his, many years previously, when quite a young man, had one Sunday evening been walking alone in the fields outside this town; and that he met a young woman, a perfect stranger, who, on some pretence asked him to see her safe home. He did so; she led him to a lone farm house, and then inviting him to walk in, shewed him into a room and left him. Whilst waiting for her return, idly looking about, he found hidden under the table, which was covered with a cloth, a dead body. On this discovery, he rushed to the door; it was locked; but the window was not very high from the ground, and by it he escaped; terrified to such a degree, that he not only left the city that very evening, but hastened out of the country, apprehensive that he had been enticed to the house and shut up with the murdered man, for the purpose of throwing the guilt on him; and as justice was not so clear sighted, and much more inexorable than in these days, he feared the circumstantial evidence might go against him. He settled in a foreign country and finally died there.

"Where this locality was, I don't know, except that it was in the environs of the city-environs which have since been covered with buildings; what if the house that we visited should have been erected on the site of that lone farm!

"It may be so; at all events, this story shews how possible it is that some similar event might have occurred on the spot where the haunted house stands."

In conclusion, let me once more recall to my readers that one, whose insight none will dispute, reminds us, in relation to this very subject, that "our philosophy," does not comprehend all wisdom and all truth. Philosophy is a good guide when she opens her eyes, but where she obstinately shuts them to one class of facts because she has previously made up her mind they cannot be genuine, she is a bad one.

Professor A. told me that when he was at Göttingen, as a great favour, and through the interest of an influential professor there, he was allowed to see a book that had belonged to Faust, or Faustus, as we call him. It was a large volume, and the leaves were stiff and hard like wood. They contained his magic rites and formulas, but on the last page was inscribed a solemn injunction to all men, as they loved their own souls, not to follow in his path or practice the teaching that volume contained.

There appears to be a mystery out of the domain—I mean the present domain of science; within the region of the hyper-psychical, regarding our relations, while in this world, with those who have past the gates, a belief in which is, I think, innate in human nature. This belief, in certain periods and places, grows rank and mischievous; at others, it is almost extinguished by reaction and education; but it never wholly dies; because, every where and in all times, circumstances have occurred to keep it alive, amongst individuals, which never reach the public ear. Now, the truth is always worth ascertaining on any subject; even this despised subject of ghosts, and those who have an inherent conviction that they themselves are spirits, temporarily clothed in flesh, feel that they have an especial interest in the question. We are fully aware that the investigation presents all sorts of difficulties, and that the belief is opposed to all sorts of accepted opinions; but we desire to ascertain the grounds of a persuasion, so nearly concerning ourselves which in all ages and all countries has prevailed in a greater or less degree, and which appears to be sustained by a vast amount of facts, which, however, we admit are not in a condition to be received as any thing beyond presumptive evidence. These facts are chiefly valuable, as furnishing cumulative testimony of the frequent recurrence of phenomena explicable by no known theory, and therefore as open to the spiritual hypothesis as any other.

When a better is offered, supported by something more convincing than pointless ridicule and dogmatic assertion, I for one, shall be ready to entertain it. In the meanwhile, hoping that time may, at length, in some degree, rend the veil that encompasses this department of psychology, we record such experiences as come under our observation and are content to await their interpretation.

Appendix

I have referred in the preceding pages to the loss of several letters, which I should have been glad to insert here.

The following very interesting ones I have fortunately retained. I give them verbatim, only suppressing the names of the writers, as requested.

Letter I

Aug. 18, 1854.

Madam,

I have received your kind favor of the 15th, and I really feel that I must now apologize to you, for venturing so quickly to call in question the accuracy of your details. Being unaware, however, of the marvellous coincidence of the *two dreams*, I feel assured you at once appreciated the motives which alone impelled me to write.

Allow me, then, to attempt a narration of the particulars referred to in my last, as having come under my own observation.

Two intimate friends of mine (clergymen of the Church of England) and one of whom is unmarried, have for the last three years occupied a large old-fashioned house in the country. It is a very pretty place-stands within its own grounds-and is quite aloof from any other dwellings. It has long had the reputation in the neighbourhood of being haunted, in consequence, it is said, of a former proprietor having committed suicide there. The story goes thus, he was *laid out* in a chamber which is now called the spare room, and is the scene of what I am about to relate. I may as well tell you that it was only on my last visit, some six weeks since, that I became at all aware of the *character* of the mansion, for my friends felt so annoyed at what has taken place, that they purposely avoided communicating to their visitors what they thought might make them anything but comfortable.

On that occasion there happened to be on a visit to my friend's wife, a lady very nearly related to him. She had the spare room assigned to her as a chamber, and on the very first night of her arrival was so terrified by what took place that she would not again sleep there without company.

She stated that in the middle of the night she was alarmed by the most unearthly groanings and lamentations-the voice seemed close to her bedside. It was afterwards attended by a rustling noise, and she distinctly felt the curtains at the foot of the bed removed. Now, as my knowledge of what was going on could not be disputed, my friends admitted that it was not the *first* time these noises had been heard, nay, that in two instances the apparition of a form in grave-clothes had been seen; the one occurring to a young gentleman of about twenty years of age, who happened to be visiting them, and the other to one of their own servants. In the former case, it appears that the young man was sitting rather late at night in the study reading-all the family being in bed-when the form emerged, apparently, from the wall dividing the study from the haunted chamber. It remained a short time only and then melted away. So great was the young man's terror that he has never been near the place since. The servant also described a similar appearance, and no one in the house who saw her terror could believe it acted. Independently of all this, no less than four gentlemen, two of them from the University, have experienced all the unearthly groanings and be-wailings before mentioned, and in nearly every instance the parties were, like myself, ignorant of the character attributed to the house. But I now come to my own experience.

I was on a visit to my friends about twelve months since, when I met a gentleman who had just left the army for the church. He appeared about 21 years of age, and there was that indescribable *something* in his manner which charmed me immediately. Without any pretence to being set up-so to speak-in piety, there was yet *that* in his sunny countenance and air of cheerfulness, which made you feel that he had been called to a brighter path of usefulness. I certainly very much admired him, and I have since learnt that he is a general favourite. On retiring to rest I found that he was to occupy the next room-not the study side.

From a variety of causes I could not sleep-but the imaginative powers were not particularly aroused-my thoughts were of very prosy and worldly things. As near as I could recollect, about an hour after I had been in bed, I heard the most dreadful groans followed by exclamations of the most horrible kind. The voice certainly *seemed* in the room, and was continued for at *least two hours*, at intervals of about ten minutes. It was that of a man who had committed a deadly sin which could never be pardoned! The agony seemed to me to be intense.

Will you believe it, Madam, in spite of what I thought of my acquaintance of the next chamber, I ascribed it to him. I believed little in the supernatural, and concluded it to be some dreadful dream. It is astonishing the thought never struck me that a *continuous* dream of such a character was scarcely possible. It did not, however, and despite of its unearthly character, and the apparent woe of the unfortunate one-the despair, as I said before, of a lost soul—I continued to associate it all with my neighbour next door, until the events which occurred at my last visit entirely upset my conviction, and I became at once assured I had been doing him a great injustice.

Like some of the cases in the "Night Side of Nature," you will perceive here a great difference in the manifestations-to some it was given to *hear*, to others to *see*. Are you still of opinion that this results from what you term comparative freedom of *rapport*! Do you not think there *are* times when the material may give place to the supernatural? I admit freely the truth of spectral illusions—I have myself experienced one-but knew it to be nothing more. Still, notwithstanding this, and my further belief in a *certain* connection of mind and matter, I cannot altogether cast from me the persuasion that the Almighty One may *at times* think fit to exercise a power independent of all rule, for the attainment of certain ends to us, perhaps, unknown.

I cannot conclude without telling you that with regard to what I have mentioned above, nothing in the shape of *trick* could possibly have been practised. Trusting I may not have trespassed too much on your patience, I will now remain, Madam, yours very respectfully,

J. H. H.

Letter II

Gloucestershire, June 10, 1854.

Madam,

Being not long ago on a visit of some days at the house of a friend, I happened to meet with your work, entitled "The Night side of Nature."

The title struck my imagination, and opening the book I was delighted to find that it treated of subjects which had long engaged my serious thoughts. I was much pleased to see in you such an able and earnest protester against the cold scepticism of the age in reference to truths of the highest order, and those too sustained by a body of evidence which in any other case would be esteemed irresistible. I must also say that I never met with so great a number of well authenticated facts in any other work as you have given us, whilst the truly catholic spirit of your theological reflections, was to me pecularly refreshing. I once had a thought of making a similar collection, that design I have however abandoned, the state of my health not admitting of much literary labour. I could relate to you many things as remarkable as any you have described, for the truth of which I can vouch. I will mention one of a most singular nature, and should you be inclined to read anything more from me on these matters, I shall feel a pleasure in the communication. Writing letters I find to be a relief from a melancholy, induced some two years ago by a variety of heavy afflictions, and this must be my apology for addressing you. But to my narrative:—

Shortly after I entered the ministry, I was introduced to a gentleman of very superior mind who belonged to the same profession, and whom I had never seen equalled for the genius and eloquence which his conversation displayed.

I became at once attached to him, and for some reason or other he evinced a desire to cultivate my friendship. After some months of most agreeable intercourse had elapsed, he was taken seriously ill, and one evening I was hastily summoned to his house. On my entering his chamber he requested that we might be left alone, and he then told me that it was his impression that his disease was mortal-that many supernatural occurrances had marked his life, which he desired might be given to the world when he was gone, and that he wished me to perform this office. Having expressed my willingness to gratify him, he commenced the chapter of extraordinaries. Here is one event in his remarkable history. Prior to his becoming a minister and when in humble circumstances, he lodged at the house of a tradesman at a certain sea-port town in W—s. He was then in perfect health. One night he retired to rest in peculiarly good spirits, and as his custom was (for it was then summer) he sat near the window and gazed for some time on the beauties of nature. He then amused himself for a while by humming a tune, when presently on looking towards the door, he saw the figure of a man enter-his dress was a blood red night cap, flannel jacket, and breeches. The man approached the bed (his countenance and walk indicating extreme illness), threw himself upon it, gave several groans and apparantly expired. My friend was so filled with horror that he lost all power of speech and motion, and remained fixed on his seat till morning, when he told his landlord the occurrence of the night, and declared that unless they could find him other apartments he would leave them that very day. The honest people were disinclined to part with him and agreed to accommodate him on the ground-floor. About *twelve months after this*, he went out on a market day for the purpose of purchasing some provisions, and when he returned, he heard that his old room was taken; but what was his surprise to find in the new lodger the very form, with the very same dress that had so terrified him a year before!

The man was then very ill: he died in a few weeks, and the circumstances were without *any exception* the same as those which my friend had witnessed. This is one of those cases in which it is extremely difficult to ascertain the design of the appearance.

I should much like to know what conjecture you would form, as to the *modus* and end of such a singular incident.

Of the veracity of the narrator it was impossible for me to doubt. As this minister is still *living* I am not at liberty to mention his name.

Pray excuse the freedom of thus addressing you, and believe me to be

Madam, with every sentiment
of respect and esteem,
Yours, very truly,
Mrs. C. Crowe. R. I. O.

Letter III

Gloucestershire, June 21, 1854.

Madam,

As I find that another communication will not be unacceptable, I proceed to detail a few cases. My first relates to the minister, a part of whose history I have given you, and belongs to the class of prophetic dreams. When he had resolved to study for the ministry and through the influence of friends, had obtained admission to a Dissenting College; as the day affixed for his departure drew near, he was filled with anxiety, from the fact that he had not even money to pay his travelling expenses.

He did not like to borrow, and he had no reason to conclude that any one suspected the miserable state of his finances. The evening before his expected removal, he laid down to rest with a troubled heart. This was in the very same seaport where the circumstance happened which I have already told you. After some hours of great mental suffering sleep came to his relief, and in his dream there seemed to approach him one of a most pleasing form, who told him that he not only saw that he was in distress, but that he well knew the cause of it, and that if he would walk down on the beach to a certain place which he pointed out as in a picture, he would find under some loose stones enough for his present necessities. In the morning, accordingly, almost as soon as it was light he hastened to the indicated spot and to his great surprise and delight found a sum amounting to a trifle more than was absolutely necessary for his journey. I would just, in passing, remark that he said that on another occasion, his father who died many years before appeared to him with an angry countenance, and assured him that he would suffer much from something he had done in reference to his family, but as this was evidently an unpleasant and even painful topic I did not wish him to enlarge upon it. The other fact I shall mention, happened to my grandfather who was also a minister. I am well aware that it is of such a nature that the relation of it would in most companies excite a burst of laughter or at least a contemptuous and sceptical smile, but I know I am addressing one who has studied in a very different school of philosophy. It was in the large town of B —m where my grandfather resided for many years, that the event took place. He himself my grandfather, my aunts, and my mother used often to tell it to their friends when the conversation turned on the supernatural. I have probably heard it a hundred times and I am not ashamed to say that on the testimony of such a man as my grandfather I cannot but yield to it my belief.

One morning when *breakfast had just commenced*, my grandfather went from the table, at which my grandmother also was sitting, into the passage, for what purpose I have now forgotten, and there he found (for the front door had been standing open,) a strange looking man in black, with a shuffling gait and a club foot. He declared that he had an instantaneous conviction that this was a supernatural appearance, and that a spirit of evil stood before him. The man in black exclaimed, moving towards the breakfast room, "I am come to take breakfast with you this morning." My grandfather convulsively seizing the handle of the door, said, with a stern look, "you are too late sir," to which the other instantly replied, "I am not too late for the remnant," and then rushed into the street. My grandfather followed, and to his amazement saw this creature at the top of the street, which was of great length, and in a moment or two he vanished. My grandmother heard a loud talking, and when my grandfather returned to the table in considerable agitation, she naturally wished to know what had occurred, but as she was near her confinement he of course concealed the matter from her. The mysterious words of the stranger followed him continually, and he puzzled himself in seeking to explain their meaning. In a few days my grandmother was confined. The child was dead-born and her life for some time hung in jeopardy. He now believed he had arrived at the solution of the difficulty-the infant was the "remnant" referred to.

I am not the subject of remarkable dreams. I had one, however, lately, and I give it you because it stands connected in my mind with the knowledge of a singular psychical fact which I am confident will greatly interest you, if you have not yet fallen upon it in the course of your reading. About a fortnight ago I thought I saw in my sleep, a young man, who is assistant to our principal surgeon, come into my room, looking exceedingly unwell. He laid himself on the other bed in my chamber, and I thought that he had come there to linger out his last illness, at which I felt not the least surprise or objection. He seemed to be perfectly resigned, and presently he began to converse with me, and after we had talked for some time, whilst he was replying to something I had said, I distinctly saw his spirit rise up out of his body. He gazed at the corpse with the deepest interest and pleasure. One moment he would stand by the head and survey the face, and the next move to the feet, and then gaze at the entire body. He called me to come and stand by his side and view this lifeless frame, which I did with as much placidity as he seemed himself to possess, and without the slightest idea of their being anything absurd in what I saw. I could not, however, help saying "O, that I could leave my body and have such a view of it as you have now of yours!" I remember no more. In the morning I had occasion to call on a friend, who has a large library containing many rare books. Not being in the humour for close reading (for I spend many hours at a time there) I took up from a centre table a volume of a lighter kind. It happened to be Mrs. Child's "Letters from New York." Turning the leaves over carelessly, my eye lighted on a chapter headed "The spirit surveying its own body!" She there says that she was told by a pious lady, that when once in a swoon, she felt that she left the body and was *standing by it* during the whole time it lasted; that she distinctly heard every word spoken by the doctor and her family, and saw every movement of their countenances, and all that was done with her body. I may observe that I have not heard that anything has occurred to the young man I saw. If I have not already tired your patience you may draw on my memory for something more. A line to that effect will oblige,

Yours, very truly,
Mrs. C. Crowe. R. I. O.

Letter IV

Edinburgh, Aug. 10th.

Madam,

In consequence of a long absence abroad, I never had, till recently, an opportunity of reading your agreeable work, "The Night side of Nature," which contains a mass of evidence in favour of your theories, to which I take the liberty of adding a few cases from my own experience.

Many years ago I lived in a house in Edinburgh, which belonged to my mother's relatives, and in which my maternal grandfather had died, several years antecedent to my own birth. The room in which I slept was that (but at the time unknown to me) in which my relative had expired. There were two beds in the room-one a large four-poster and the other a sort of couch. The latter was next the door, and both lay between it and the window, which was barred and bolted, and opposite to them was the fireplace, with rather a high mantlepiece. Being summer, the "board" was on the chimney. It was about eleven o'clock at night; the rest of the family had retired to rest. As there were only about two inches of candle left, I placed the candlestick on the mantlepiece, intending to allow it to burn out, and went to my bed, which was on the couch. I had just lain down, and was looking towards the candle, when, to my extreme horror, I perceived a tall old man in his night dress, standing by the mantlepiece. His sight seemed impaired, for he put forth his hand *and felt for something*, and then moved across the fireplace, in doing which, *he obscured the light on passing it.* My gaze was riveted on him. He then turned towards the large bed on my left, and stretching out his hands attempted with a feeble effort to lay himself down, and in doing so I heard him *sigh* distinctly. He disappeared almost at the same moment. He did not appear to have noticed me. I immediately sprang out of bed and opening the door on my right hand, called out loudly, but *never left the doorway*, as I was resolved that if the figure were that of a living person there should be no means of egress. On the assembling of the family in my room, a search was made; but there was nothing to be seen, and there had been no possibility of a human being having been in the room; the affair was put down to an *illusion*. Yet so strong an impression did it leave on my mind, that a few years since (1851 or 52), when in India, I published in "Saunder's Magazine," printed at the Delhi Gazette press, an account of this apparition, in a narrative, which I wrote called "Idone, or Incidents in the life of a dreamer," and which with the exception of this introductory vision, was, in reality, a series of actual dreams of which I had kept a record, and this I endeavoured to weave into a vague story, with the view of illustrating how a person might live *two distinct lives*!

Sometime after the above were published, I read with much interest, "Swedenborg's Theory of the Spiritual World;" and lately when reading your work, I was struck with some peculiar resemblances between my own experience and the cases you cite.

But to return to the family and house in Edinburgh, of my grandfather. Other members of the family have seen unaccountable figures in the same house. An aunt of mine and a cousin, one night, met an old woman on the stairs with a large bunch of keys, and were in the greatest alarm. On another occasion, on going to open a room which had been locked up for some time, in order to prepare it for the reception of my eldest uncle, who had just returned that night from abroad, two members of the family started back and locked the door again, for on entering they had both seen the *mattrass &c. violently heaved up*. On returning with the servants, nothing was visible of an unusual description. Again, two relatives occupied the same room, and one night, as the fire was burning low, after they had gone to bed (the door being locked) they were alarmed by a sound like wings, over their beds, and by a *dusky form* moving about the room. It walked up to the fireplace and seemed restless. When it had disappeared, they both rose and *unlocked* the door, called for assistance, but, as usual, nothing of their visitor was to be seen. A still more remarkable incident occurred in the same house. As two of my aunts were sitting opposite the window, at night, they were startled by the apparition of an absent brother-in-law looking in, and with a pen in his hand. A few days afterwards the intelligence of his death arrived. He had been *signing his will* at the exact time they had seen his apparation. My eldest uncle shortly after his return from abroad went to Musselburgh to visit an old school-master, and as he entered the yard he observed him limping into the school. He tried to overtake him, and on reaching the door he met one of the tutors, who informed him that the Dr. had been confined to his bed for some time with a broken leg.

The same uncle, who was an officer in the army, dreamt that he had obtained his captaincy by the retirement of an officer of the name of Patterson (so far as I remember.) There was no such officer then in the regiment, and he mentioned it as strange that he should have dreamt of a *particular* name. A few Gazettes afterwards my uncle obtained his promotion by an officer of *this* name being *brought in from the half-pay to sell out in the same Gazette.*

I have myself heard the most remarkable and unaccountable noises in my grandfather's house. The servants were often in the greatest terror. I have heard, seemingly, the whole of the furniture, in a particular room, thrown violently about, accompanied with the noise of something rolling on the floor. At other times I have distinctly heard, as it were, a boy's marble falling step by step down the stairs and striking against my door, which was at the foot of them, and yet this was at night, and there were no children in the house. This annoyance, with that of steps heard round my bed, was so common as to cease to make any impression on me.

I may mention that my grandfather was not happy in his family relations, and died in an uneasy frame of mind, on Christmas eve, 1820. Since my family sold his house, I have never heard that its new occupants were disturbed.

I have at different periods of my life had *groups*, as it were, of very remarkable allegorical dreams.

It is somewhat singular that involuntary efforts may be made during sleep, which are I believe beyond the bounds of possibility during waking moments. Indeed the curious phenomena which you have so ably criticised, are without limit.

Though you do not approve of the concealment of names, I hope you will excuse my asking you to do so in the present instance as many of the parties concerned might be displeased.

I have the honour to remain,
Madam,
Your obedient servant,
Mrs. Catherine Crowe. H. A.

"P.S. I know two remarkable instances of prophetic denunciation or the power of will, under, of course, the control of Providence. In one instance, the death of the party denounced, followed on the week predicted, although at the time he was well. Moreover, the denunciation was never mentioned to him.

"In the other instance, the accomplishment of the denunciation was accomplished to the exact day, and under very remarkable circumstances. I believe this power to be *involuntary*, and more of the nature of inspiration."

Second Part
Legends of the Earthbound

The Italian's Story

"How well your friend speaks English!" I remarked one day to an acquaintance when I was abroad, alluding to a gentleman who had just quitted the room. "What is his name?"

"Count Francesco Ferraldi."

"I suppose he has been in England?"

"Oh, yes; he was exiled and taught Italian there. His history is very curious and would interest you, who like wonderful things."

"Can you tell it me."

"Not correctly, as I never heard it from himself. But I believe he has no objection to tell it-with the exception of the political transactions in which he was concerned, and which caused his being sent out of the Austrian dominions; that part of it I believe he thinks it prudent not to allude to. We'll ask him to dinner, if you'll meet him, and perhaps we may persuade him to tell the story."

Accordingly, the meeting took place; we dined *en petit comité*, —and the Count very good-naturedly yielded to our request; "but you must excuse me," he said, "beginning a long way back for my story commences three hundred years ago.

"Our family claims to be of great antiquity, but we were not very wealthy till about the latter half of the 16th century, when Count Jacopo Ferraldi made very considerable additions to the property; not only by getting, but also by saving-he was in fact a miser. Before that period the Ferraldis had been warriors, and we could boast of many distinguished deeds of arms recorded in our annals; but Jacopo, although by the death of his brother, he ultimately inherited the title and the estates, had begun life as a younger son, and being dissatisfied with his portion, had resolved to increase it by commerce.

"Florence then was a very different city to what it is now; trade flourished, and its merchants had correspondence and large dealings with all the chief cities of Europe. My ancestor invested his little fortune so judiciously, or so fortunately, that he trebled it in his first venture; and as people grow rapidly rich who gain and don't spend, he soon had wealth to his heart's content-but I am wrong in using that term as applied to him-he was never content with his gains but still worked on to add to them, for he grew to love the money for itself, and not for what it might purchase.

"At length, his two elder brothers died, and as they left no issue he succeeded to their inheritance, and dwelt in the palace of his ancestors; but instead of circulating his riches he hoarded them; and being too miserly to entertain his friends and neighbours, he lived like an anchorite in his splendid halls, exulting in his possessions but never enjoying them. His great pleasure and chief occupation seems to have been counting his money, which he kept either hidden in strange out-of-the-way places, or in strong iron chests, clamped to the floors and walls. But notwithstanding those precautions and that he guarded it like a watch dog, to his great dismay he one day missed a sum of two thousand pounds which he had concealed in an ingeniously contrived receptacle under the floor of his dining-room, the existence of which was only known to the man who made it; at least, so he believed. Small as was this sum in proportion to what he possessed, the shock was tremendous; he rushed out of his house like a madman with the intention of dragging the criminal to justice, but when he arrived at the man's shop he found him in bed and at the point of death. His friends and the doctor swore that he had not quitted it for a fortnight; in short, according to their shewing, he was taken ill on his return from working at the Count's, the very day he finished the job.

"If this were true, he could not be the thief, as the money was not deposited there till some days afterwards, and although the Count had his doubts, it was not easy to disprove what everybody swore, more especially as the man died on the following day, and was buried. Baffled and furious, he next fell foul of his two servants-he kept but two, for he only inhabited a small part of the palace. There was not the smallest reason to suspect them, nor to suppose they knew anything of the hiding place, for every precaution had been used to conceal it; moreover, he had found it locked as he himself had locked it after depositing the money, and he was quite sure the key had never been absent from his own person. Nevertheless, he discharged them and took no others. The thief, whoever he was, had evinced so much ingenuity, that he trembled to think what such skill might compass with opportunity. So he resolved to afford none; and henceforth to have his meals sent in from a neighbouring eating-house, and to have a person once a week to sweep and clean his rooms, whom he could keep an eye on while it was doing. As he had no clue to the perpetrators of the robbery, and the man whom he had most reason to suspect was dead, he took no further steps in the business, but kept it quiet lest he should draw too much attention towards his secret hoards; nevertheless, though externally calm, the loss preyed upon his mind and caused him great anguish.

"Shortly after this occurrence, he received a letter from a sister of his who had several years before married an Englishman, saying that her husband was dead, and it being advisable that her dear and only son should enter into commerce, that she was going to send him to Florence, feeling assured that her brother would advise him for the best, and enable him to employ the funds he brought with him advantageously.

"This was not pleasing intelligence; he did not want to promote any body's interest but his own, and he felt that the young man would be a spy on his actions, an intruder in his house, and no doubt an expectant and greedy heir, counting the hours till he died; for this sister and her family were his nearest of kin, and would inherit if he left no will to the contrary. However, his arrival could not be prevented; letters travelled slowly in those days, and ere his could reach England his nephew would have quitted it, so he resolved to give him a cold reception and send him back as soon as he could.

"In the mean time, the young man had started on his journey, full of hope and confidence, and immediately on his arrival hastened to present himself to this rich uncle who was to shew him the path he had himself followed to fortune. It was not for his own sake alone he coveted riches, but his mother and sister were but poorly provided for, and they had collected the whole of their little fortune and risked it upon this venture, hoping, with the aid of their relative, to be amply repaid for the present sacrifice.

"A fine open countenanced lad was Arthur Allen, just twenty years of age; such a face and figure had not beamed upon those old halls for many a day. Well brought up and well instructed too; he spoke Italian as well as English, his mother having accustomed him to it from infancy.

"Though he had heard his uncle was a miser, he had no conception of the amount to which the mania had arisen; and his joyous anticipations were somewhat damped when he found himself so coldly received, and when he looked into those hard grey eyes and contracted features that had never expanded with a genial smile; so fearing the old man might be apprehensive that he had come as an applicant for assistance to set him up in trade, he hastened to inform him of the true state of the case, saying that they had got together two thousand pounds.

"'Of course, my mother,' he said, 'would not have entrusted my inexperience with such a sum; but she desired me to place it in your hands, and to act entirely under your direction.

"To use the miser's own expression-for we have learnt all these particulars from a memoir left by himself—'When I heard these words the devil entered into me, and I bade the youth bring the money and dine with me on the following day.'

"I daresay you will think the devil had entered into him long before; however, now he recognized his presence, but that did not deter him from following his counsel.

"Pleased that he had so far thawed his uncle's frigidity, Arthur arrived the next day with his money bags at the appointed hour, and was received in an inner chamber; their contents were inspected and counted, and then placed in one of the old man's iron chests. Soon afterwards the tinkle of a bell announced that the waiter from the neighbouring traiteur's had brought the dinner, and the host left the room to see that all was ready. Presently he re-entered, and led his guest to the table. The repast was not sumptuous, but there was a bottle of old Lacryma Christi which he much recommended, and which the youth tasted with great satisfaction. But strange! He had no sooner swallowed the first glass, than his eyes began to stare-there was a gurgle in his throat—a convulsion passed over his face-and his body stiffened.

"'I did not look up,' says the old man in his memoir, 'for I did not like to see the face of the boy that had sat down so hearty to his dinner, so I kept on eating mine-but I heard the gurgle, and I knew what had happened; and presently lest the servant should come to fetch the dinner things, I pushed the table aside and opened the receptacle from which my two thousand pounds had been stolen-curses on the thief! and I laid the body in it, and the wine therewith. I locked it and drove in two strong nails. Then I put back the table-moved away the lad's chair and plate, unlocked the door which was fast, and sat down to finish my dinner. I could not help chuckling as I ate, to think how his had been spoilt.

"'I closed up that apartment, as I thought there might be a smell that would raise observation, and I selected one on the opposite side of the gallery for my dining-room. All went well till the following day. I counted my two thousand pounds again and again, and I kept gloating over the recovery of it-for I felt as if it was my own money, and that I had a right to seize it where I could. I wrote also to my sister, saying, that her son had not arrived; but that when he did, I would do my best to forward his views. My heart was light that day-they say that's a bad sign.

"'Yes, all was so far well; but the next day we were two of us at dinner! And yet I had invited no guest; and the next and the next, and so on always! As I was about to sit down, he entered and took a chair opposite me, an unbidden guest. I ceased dining at home, but it made no difference; he came, dine where I would. This preyed upon me; I tried not to mind, but I could not help it. Argument was vain. I lost my appetite, and was reduced nearly to death's door. At last, driven to desperation, I consulted Fra Guiseppe. He had been a fast fellow in his time, and it was said had been too impatient for his father's succession; howbeit, the old man died suddenly; Guiseppe spent the money and then took to religion. I thought he was a proper person to consult, so I told him my case. He recommended repentance and restitution. I tried, but I could not repent, for I had got the money; but I thought, perhaps, if I parted with it to another, I might be released; so I looked about for an advantageous purchase, and hearing that Bartolomeo Malfi was in difficulties, I offered him two thousand pounds, money down, for his land—I knew it was worth three times the sum. We signed the agreement, and then I went home and opened the door of the room where it was; but lo! he sat there upon the chest where the money was fast locked, and I could not get it. I peeped in two or three times, but he was always there; so I was obliged to expend other moneys in this purchase, which vexed me, albeit the bargain was a good one. Then I consulted friend Guiseppe again, and he said nothing would do but restitution-but that was hard, so I waited; and I said to myself, I'll eat and care not whether he sit there or no. But woe be to him! he chilled the marrow of my bones, and I could not away with him; so I said one day, "What if I go to England with the money?" and he bowed his head.'

"The old man accordingly took the moneybags from the chest and started for England. His sister and her daughter were still living in the house they had inhabited during the husband's lifetime; in short, it was their own; and being attached to the place they hoped, if the young man succeeded in his undertakings, to be able to keep it. It was a small house with a garden full of flowers, which the ladies cultivated themselves. The village church was close at hand, and the churchyard adjoined the garden. The poor ladies had become very uneasy at not hearing of Arthur's arrival; and when the old man presented himself and declared he had never seen anything of him, great was their affliction and dismay; for it was clear that either some misfortune had happened to the boy, or he had appropriated the money and gone off in some other direction. They scarcely admitted the possibility of the last contingency, although it was the one their little world universally adopted, in spite of his being a very well conducted and affectionate youth; but people said it was too great a temptation for his years, and blamed his mother for entrusting him with so much money. Whichever it was, the blow fell very heavy on them in all ways, for Arthur was their sole stay and support, and they loved him dearly.

"Since he had set out on this journey, the old man had been relieved from the company of his terrible guest, and was beginning to recover himself a little, but it occasioned him a severe pang when he remembered that this immunity was to be purchased with the sacrifice of two thousand pounds, and he set himself to think how he could jockey the ghost. But while he was deliberating on this subject, an event happened that alarmed him for the immediate safety of the money.

"He had found on the road, that the great weight of a certain chest he brought with him, had excited observation whenever his luggage had to be moved; on his arrival two labouring men had been called in to carry it into the house, and he had overheard some remarks that induced him to think they had drawn a right conclusion with regard to its contents. Subsequently, he saw these two men hovering about the house in a suspicious manner, and he was afraid to leave it or to go to sleep at night, lest he should be robbed.

"So far we learn from Jocopo Ferraldi himself; but there the memoir stops. Tradition says that he was found one morning murdered in his bed and his chest rifled. All the family, that is the mother and daughter and their one servant, were accused of the murder; and notwithstanding their protestation of innocence were declared guilty and executed.

"The memoir I have quoted was found on his dressing table, and he appears to have been writing it when he was surprised by the assassins; for the last words were —'I think I've baulked them, and nobody will understand the —' then comes a large blot and a mark, as if the pen had fallen out of his hand. It seems wonderful that this man, so suspicious and secretive, should thus have entrusted to paper what it was needful he should conceal; but the case is not singular; it has been remarked in similar instances, when some dark mystery is pressing on a human soul, that there exists an irresistible desire to communicate it, notwithstanding the peril of betrayal; and when no other confident can be found, the miserable wretch has often had recourse to paper.

"The family of Arthur Allen being now extinct, a cousin of Jacopo's, who was a penniless soldier, succeeded to the title and estate, and the memoir, with a full account of what had happened, being forwarded to Italy, enquiries were made about the missing two thousand pounds; but it was not forthcoming; and it was at first supposed that the ladies had had some accomplice who had carried it off. Subsequently, however, one of the two men who had borne the money chest into the house, at the period of the old man's arrival, was detected in endeavouring to dispose of some Italian gold coin and a diamond ring, which Jacopo was in the habit of wearing. This led to investigation, and he ultimately confessed to the murder committed by himself and his companion, thus exonerating the unfortunate woman. He nevertheless declared that they had not rifled the strong box, as they could not open it, and were disturbed by the barking of a dog before they could search for the keys. The box itself they were afraid to carry away, it being a remarkable one and liable to attract notice; and that therefore their only booty was some loose coin and some jewels that were found on the old man's person. But this was not believed, especially as his accomplice was not to be found, and appeared, on enquiry, to have left that part of the country immediately after the catastrophe.

"There the matter rested for nearly two centuries and a half. Nobody sorrowed for Jacopo Ferraldi, and the fate of the Allens was a matter of indifference to the public, who was glad to see the estate fall into the hands of his successor, who appears to have made a much better use of his riches. The family in the long period that elapsed, had many vicissitudes; but at the period of my birth my father inhabited the same old palace, and we were in tolerably affluent circumstances. I was born there, and I remember as a child the curiosity I used to feel about the room with the secret receptacle under the floor where Jacopo had buried the body of his guest. It had been found there and received Christian burial; but the receptacle still remained, and the room was shut up being said to be haunted. I never *saw* anything extraordinary, but I can bear witness to the frightful groans and moans that issued from it sometimes at night, when, if I could persuade anybody to accompany me, I used to stand in the gallery and listen with wonder and awe. But I never passed the door alone, nor would any of the servants do so after dark. There had been an attempt made to exclude the sounds by walling up the door; but so far from this succeeding they became twenty times worse, and as the wall was a disfigurement as well as a failure, the unquiet spirit was placated by taking it down again.

"The old man's memoir is always preserved amongst the family papers, and his picture still hangs in the gallery. Many strangers who have heard something of this extraordinary story, have asked to see it. The palace is now inhabited by an Austrian nobleman,—whether the ghost continues to annoy the inmates by his lamentations I do not know.

"'I now,' said Count Francesco, 'come to my personal history. Political reasons a few years since obliged me to quit Italy with my family. I had no resources except a little ready money that I had brought with me, and I had resolved to utilise some musical talent which I had cultivated for my amusement. I had not voice enough to sing in public, but I was capable of giving lessons and was considered, when in Italy, a successful amateur. I will not weary you with the sad details of my early residence in England; you can imagine the difficulties that an unfortunate foreigner must encounter before he can establish a connexion. Suffice it to say that my small means were wholly exhausted, and that very often I, and what was worse, my wife and child were in want of bread, and indebted to one of my more prosperous countrymen for the very necessaries of life. I was almost in despair, and I do not know what rash thing I might have done if I had been a single man; but I had my family depending on me, and it was my duty not to sink under my difficulties however great they were.

"One night I had been singing at the house of a nobleman, in St. James's Square, and had received some flattering compliments from a young man who appeared to be very fond of Italian music, and to understand it. My getting to this party was a stroke of good luck in the first instance, for I was quite unknown to the host, but Signor A. an acquaintance of mine, who had been engaged for the occasion, was taken ill at the last moment, and had sent me with a note of introduction to supply his place.

"I knew, of course, that I should be well paid for my services, but I would have gladly accepted half the sum I expected if I could have had it that night, for our little treasury was wholly exhausted, and we had not sixpence to purchase a breakfast for the following day. When the great hall door shut upon me, and I found myself upon the pavement, with all that luxury and splendour on one side, and I and my desolation on the other, the contrast struck me cruelly, for I too had been rich, and dwelt in illuminated palaces, and had a train of liveried servants at my command, and sweet music had echoed through my halls. I felt desperate, and drawing my hat over my eyes I began pacing the square, forming wild plans for the relief or escape from my misery. No doubt I looked frantic; for you know we Italians have such a habit of gesticulating, that I believe my thoughts were accompanied by movements that must have excited notice; but I was too much absorbed to observe anything, till I was roused by a voice saying, 'Signor Ferraldi, still here this damp chilly night! Are you not afraid for your voice-it is worth taking care of.'

"'To what purpose,' I said savagely, 'It will not give me bread!'

"If the interruption had not been so sudden, I should not have made such an answer, but I was surprised into it before I knew who had addressed me. When I looked up I saw it was the young man I had met at Lord L.'s, who had complimented me on my singing. I took off my hat and begged his pardon, and was about to move away, when he took my arm.

"'Excuse me,' he said, 'let us walk together,' and then after a little pause, he added, with an apology, 'I think you are an exile.'

"'I am,' I said.

"'And I think,' he continued, 'I have surprised you out of a secret that you would not voluntarily have told me. I know well the hardships that beset many of your countrymen-as good gentlemen as we are ourselves-when you are obliged to leave your country; and I beg therefore you will not think me impertinent or intrusive, if I beg you to be frank with me and tell me how you are situated!'

"This offer of sympathy was evidently so sincere, and it was so welcome, at such a moment, that I did not hesitate to comply with my new friend's request—I told him everything-adding that in time I hoped to get known, and that then I did not fear being able to make my way; but that meanwhile we were in danger of starving.

"During this conversation we were walking round and round the square, where in fact he lived. Before we parted at his own door, he had persuaded me to accept of a gift, I call it, for he had then no reason to suppose I should ever be able to repay him, but he called it an advance of ten guineas upon some lessons I was to give him; the first instalment of which was to be paid the following day.

"I went home with a comparitively light heart, and the next morning waited on my friendly pupil, whom I found, as I expected, a very promising scholar. He told me with a charming frankness, that he had not much influence in fashionable society, for his family, though rich, was *parvenue*, but he said he had two sisters, as fond of music as himself, who would be shortly in London, and would be delighted to take lessons, as I had just the voice they liked to sing with them.

"This was the first auspicious incident that had occurred to me, nor did the omen fail in its fulfilment. I received great kindness from the family when they came to London. I gave them lessons, sung at their parties, and they took every opportunity of recommending me to their friends.

"When the end of the season approached, however, I felt somewhat anxious about the future-there would be no parties to sing at, and my pupils would all be leaving town; but my new friends, whose name, by the way, was Greathead, had a plan for me in their heads, which they strongly recommended me to follow. They said they had a house in the country with a large neighbourhood-in fact, near a large watering-place; and that if I went there during the summer months, they did not doubt my getting plenty of teaching; adding, 'We are much greater people there than we are here, you see; and our recommendation will go a great way.'

"I followed my friend's advice, and soon after they left London, I joined them at Salton, which was the name of their place. As I had left my wife and children in town, with very little money, I was anxious that they should join me as soon as possible; and therefore the morning after my arrival, I proceeded to look for a lodging at S., and to take measures to make my object known to the residents and visitors there. My business done, I sent my family directions for their journey, and then returned to Salton to spend a few days, as I had promised my kind patrons.

"The house was modern, in fact it had been built by Mr. Greathead's grandfather, who was the architect of their fortunes; the grounds were extensive, and the windows looked on a fine lawn, a picturesque ruin, a sparkling rivulet, and a charming flower-garden; there could not be a prettier view than that we enjoyed while sitting at breakfast. It was my first experience of the lovely and graceful English homes, and it fully realised all my expectations, both within doors and without. After breakfast Mr. Greathead and his son asked me to accompany them round the grounds, as they were contemplating some alterations.

"'Among other things,' said Mr. G., 'we want to turn this rivulet; but my wife has a particular fancy for that old hedge, which is exactly in the way, and she won't let me root it up.'

"The hedge alluded to enclosed two sides of the flower-garden, but seemed rather out of place, I thought.

"'Why?' said I. 'What is Mrs. Greathead's attachment to the hedge?'

"'Why? it's very old; it formerly bordered the churchyard, for that old ruin you see there, is all that remains of the parish church; and this flower-garden, I fancy, is all the more brilliant for the rich soil of the burial-ground. But what is remarkable is, that the hedge and that side of the garden are full of Italian flowers, and always have been so as long as anybody can remember. Nobody knows how it happens, but they must spring up from some old seeds that have been long in the ground. Look at this cyclamen growing wild in the hedge.'

"The subject of the alterations was renewed at dinner, and Mrs. Greathead, still objecting to the removal of the hedge, her younger son, whose name was Harry, said, 'It is very well for mamma to pretend it is for the sake of the flowers, but I am quite sure that the real reason is that she is afraid of offending the ghost.'

"'What nonsence, Harry,' she said. 'You must not believe him, Mr. Ferraldi.'

"'Well mamma,' said the boy, 'you know you will never be convinced that that was not a ghost you saw.'

"'Never mind what it was,' she said; 'I won't have the hedge removed. Presently,' she added, 'I suppose you would laugh at the idea of anybody believing in a ghost, Mr. Ferraldi.'

"'Quite the contrary,' I answered; 'I believe in them myself, and upon very good grounds, for we have a celebrated ghost in our family.'

"'Well,' she said, 'Mr. Greathead and the boys laugh at me; but when I came to live here, upon the death of Mr. Greathead's grandfather, —for his father never inhabited the place, having died by an accident before the old gentleman, —I had never heard a word of the place being haunted; and, perhaps, I should not have believed it if I had. But, one evening, when the younger children were gone to bed, and Mr. Greathead and George were sitting with some friends in the dining-room, I, and my sister, who was staying with me, strolled into the garden. It was in the month of August, and a bright starlight night. We were talking on a very interesting matter, for my sister had that day, received an offer from the gentleman she afterwards married. I mention that, to show you that we were not thinking of anything supernatural, but, on the contrary, that our minds were quite absorbed with the subject we were discussing. I was looking on the ground, as one often does, when listening intently to what another person is saying; my sister was speaking, when she suddenly stopped, and laid her hand on my arm, saying, 'Who's that?'

"'I raised my eyes and saw, not many yards from us, an old man, withered and thin, dressed in a curious antique fashion, with a high peaked hat on his head. I could not conceive who he could be, or what he could be doing there, for it was close to the flower-garden; so we stood still to observe him. I don't know whether you saw the remains of an old tombstone in a corner of the garden? It is said to be that of a former rector of the parish; the date, 1550, is still legible upon it. The old man walked from one side of the hedge to that stone, and seemed to be counting his steps. He walked like a person pacing the ground, to measure it; then he stopped, and appeared to be noting the result of his measurement with a pencil and paper he held in his hand; then he did the same thing, the other side of the hedge, pacing up to the tombstone and back.

"'There was a talk, at that time, of removing the hedge, and digging up the old tombstone; and it occurred to me, that my husband might have been speaking to somebody about it, and that this man might be concerned in the business, though, still, his dress and appearance puzzled me. It seemed odd, too, that he took no notice of us; and I might have remarked, that we heard no footsteps, though we were quite close enough to do so; but these circumstances did not strike me then. However, I was just going to advance, and ask him what he was doing? when I felt my sister's hand relax the hold she had of my arm, and she sank to the ground; at the same instant I lost sight of the mysterious old man, who suddenly disappeared.

"'My sister had not fainted; but she said her knees had bent under her, and she had slipt down, collapsed by terror. I did not feel very comfortable myself, I assure you; but I lifted her up, and we hastened back to the house and told what we had seen. The gentlemen went out, and, of course, saw nothing, and laughed at us; but shortly afterwards, when Harry was born, I had a nurse from the village, and she asked me one day, if I had ever happened to see "the old gentleman that walks!" I had ceased to think of the circumstance, and inquired what old gentleman she meant? and then she told me that, long ago, a foreign gentleman had been murdered here; that is, in the old house that Mr. Greathead's grandfather pulled down when he built this; and that, ever since, the place has been haunted, and that nobody will pass by the hedge, and the old tombstone after dark; for that is the spot to which the ghost confines himself.'

"'But I should think,' said I, 'that so far from desiring to preserve these objects, you would rather wish them removed, since the ghost would, probably, cease to visit the spot at all.'

"'Quite the contrary,' answered Mrs. G. 'The people of the neighbourhood say, that the former possessor of the place entertained the same idea, and had resolved to remove them; but that then, the old man became very troublesome, and was even seen in the house; the nurse positively assured me, that her mother had told her, old Mr. Greathead had also intended to remove them; but that he quite suddenly counter-ordered the directions he had given, and, though he did not confess to anything of the sort, the people all believed that he had seen the ghost. Certain, it is, that this hedge has always been maintained by the proprietors of the place.'

"The young men laughed and quizzed their mother for indulging in such superstitions; but the lady was quite firm in her opposition, alledging, that independently of all considerations connected with the ghost, she liked the hedge on account of the wild Italian flowers; and she liked the old tombstone on account of its antiquity.

"Consequently, some other plan was devised for Mr. Greathead's alterations, which led the course of the rivulet quite clear of the hedge and the tombstone.

"In a few days, my family arrived, and I established myself at S., for the summer. The speculation answered very well, and through the recommendations of Mr. and Mrs. Greathead, and their personal kindness to myself and my wife, we passed the time very pleasantly. When the period for our returning to London approached, they invited us to spend a fortnight with them before our departure, and, accordingly, the day we gave up our lodgings, we removed to Salton.

"Preparations for turning the rivulet had then commenced; and soon after my arrival, I walked out with Mr. Greathead to see the works. There was a boy, about fourteen, amongst the labourers; and while we were standing close to him, he picked up something, and handed it to Mr. G., saying, 'Is this yours, sir?' which, on examination, proved to be a gold coin of the sixteenth century,—the date on it was 1545. Presently, the boy who was digging, picked up another, and then several more.

"'This becomes interesting,' said Mr. Greathead, 'I think we are coming upon some buried treasure;' and he whispered to me, that he had better not leave the spot.

"Accordingly, he did stay, till it was time to dress for dinner; and, feeling interested, I remained also. In the interval, many more coins were found; and when he went in, he dismissed the workmen, and sent a servant to watch the place,—for he saw by their faces, that if he had not happened to be present he would, probably, never have heard of the circumstance. A few more turned up the following day, and then the store seemed exhausted. When the villagers heard of this money being discovered, they all looked upon it as the explanation of the old gentleman haunting that particular spot. No doubt he had buried the money, and it remained to be seen, whether now, that it was found, his spirit would be at rest.

"My two children were with me at Salton on this occasion. They slept in a room on the third floor, and one morning, my wife having told me that the younger of the two seemed unwell, I went up stairs to look at her. It was a cheerful room, with two little white beds in it, and several old prints and samplers, and bits of work such as you see in nurseries, framed and hung against the wall. After I had spoken to the child, and while my wife was talking to the maid, I stood with my hands in my pockets, idly looking at these things. Amongst them was one that arrested my attention, because at first I could not understand it, nor see why this discoloured parchment, with a few lines and dots on it, should have been framed and glazed. There were some words here and there which I could not decipher; so I lifted the frame off the nail and carried it to the window. Then I saw that the words were Italian, written in a crabbed, old-fashioned hand, and the whole seemed to be a plan, or sketch, rudely drawn, of what I at first thought was a camp-but, on closer examination, I saw was part of a churchyard, with tomb stones, from one of which lines were drawn to various dots, and along these lines were numbers, and here and there a word as *right*, *left*, &c. There were also two lines forming a right angle, which intersected the whole, and after contemplating the thing for some time, it struck me that it was a rude sort of map of the old churchyard and the hedge, which had formed the subject of conversation some days before.

"At breakfast, I mentioned what I had observed to Mr. and Mrs. Greathead, and they said they believed it was; it had been found when the old house was pulled down, and was kept on account of its antiquity.

"'Of what period is it,' I asked, 'and how happens it to have been made by an Italian?'

"'The last question I can't answer,' said Mr. Greathead; 'but the date is on it, I believe.'

"'No,' said I, 'I examined it particularly-there is no date.'

"'Oh, there is a date and name, I think-but I never examined it myself;' and to settle the question he desired his son Harry to run up and fetch it, adding, 'you know Italian architects and designers of various kinds, were not rare in this country a few centuries ago.'

"Harry brought the frame, and we were confirmed in our conjectures of what it represented, but we could find no date or name.

"'And yet I think I've heard there was one,' said Mr. Greathead. 'Let us take it out of the frame?'

"This was easily done, and we found the date and the name; the count paused, and then added, 'I dare say you can guess it?'

"'Jacopo Ferraldi?' I said.

"'It was,' he answered; and it immediately occurred to me that he had buried the money supposed to have been stolen on the night he was murdered, and that this was a plan to guide him in finding it again. So I told Mr. Greathead the story I have now told you, and mentioned my reasons for supposing that if I was correct in my surmise, more gold would be found.

"With the old man's map as our guide, we immediately set to work-the whole family vigorously joining in the search; and, as I expected, we found that the tombstone in the garden was the point from which all the lines were drawn, and that the dots indicated where the money lay. It was in different heaps, and appeared to have been enclosed in bags, which had rotted away with time. We found the whole sum mentioned in the memoir, and Mr. Greathead being lord of the manor, was generous enough to make it all over to me, as being the lawful heir, which, however, I certainly was not, for it was the spoil of a murderer and a thief, and it properly belonged to the Allens. But that family had become extinct; at least, so we believed, when the two unfortunate ladies were executed, and I accepted the gift with much gratitude and a quiet conscience. It relieved us from our pressing difficulties, and enabled me to wait for better times.

"'And,' said I, 'how of the ghost? was he pleased or otherwise, by the *denouement*?'

"'I cannot say,' replied the count; 'I have not heard of his being seen since; I understand, however, that the villagers, who understand these things better than we do, say, that they should not be surprised if he allowed the hedge and tombstone to be removed now without opposition; but Mr. Greathead, on the contrary, wished to retain them as mementoes of these curious circumstances.'"

The Dutch Officer's Story

"Well, I think nothing can be so cowardly as to be afraid to own the truth?" said the pretty Madame de B., an Englishwoman, who had married a Dutch officer of distinction.

"Are you really venturing to accuse the General of cowardice?" said Madame L.

"Yes," said Madame de B., "I want him to tell Mrs. Crowe a ghost story—a thing that he saw himself-and he pooh, poohs it, though he owned it to me before we were married, and since too, saying that he never could have believed such a thing if he had not seen it himself."

While the wife was making this little *tirade*, the husband looked as if she was accusing him of picking somebody's pocket—*il perdait contenance* quite. "Now, look at him," she said, "don't you see guilt in his face, Mrs. Crowe?"

"Decidedly," I answered; "so experienced a seeker of ghost stories as myself cannot fail to recognise the symptoms. I always find that when the circumstances is mere hearsay, and happened to nobody knows who, people are very ready to tell it; when it has happened to one of their own family, they are considerably less communicative, and will only tell it under protest; but when they are themselves the parties concerned, it is the most difficult thing imaginable to induce them to relate the thing seriously, and with its details; they say they have forgotten it, and don't believe it; and as an evidence of their incredulity, they affect to laugh at the whole affair. If the General will tell me the story, I shall think it quite as decisive a proof of courage as he ever gave in the field."

Betwixt bantering and persuasion, we succeeded in our object, and the General began as follows:—

"You know the Belgian Rebellion (he always called it so) took place in 1830. It broke out at Brussels on the 28th of August, and we immediately advanced with a considerable force to attack that city; but as the Prince of Orange hoped to bring the people to reason, without bloodshed, we encamped at Vilvorde, whilst he entered Brussels alone, to hold a conference with the armed people. I was a Lieutenant-Colonel then, and commanded the 20th foot, to which regiment I had been lately appointed.

"We had been three or four days in cantonment, when I heard two of the men, who were digging a little drain at the back of my tent, talking of Jokel Falck, a private in my regiment, who was noted for his extraordinary disposition to somnolence, one of them remarked that he would certainly have got into trouble for being asleep on his post the previous night, if it had not been for Mungo. 'I don't know how many times he has saved him,' added he.

"To which the other answered, that Mungo was a very valuable friend, and had saved many a man from punishment.

"This was the first time I had ever heard of Mungo, and I rather wondered who it was they alluded to; but the conversation slipt from my mind and I never thought of asking any body.

"Shortly after this I was going my rounds, being field-officer of the day, when I saw by the moonlight, the sentry at one of the outposts stretched upon the ground. I was some way off when I first perceived him; and I only knew what the object was from the situation, and because I saw the glitter of his accoutrements; but almost at the same moment that I discovered him, I observed a large black Newfoundland dog trotting towards him. The man rose as the dog approached, and had got upon his legs before I reached the spot. This occupied the space of about two minutes-perhaps, not so much.

"'You were asleep on your post,' I said; and turning to the mounted orderly that attended me, I told him to go back and bring a file of the guard to take him prisoner, and to send a sentry to relieve him.

"'Non, mon colonel,' said he, and from the way he spoke I perceived he was intoxicated, 'it's all the fault of that *damné* Mungo. Il m'a manqué.'

"But I paid no attention to what he said and rode on, concluding *Mungo* was some slang term of the men for drink.

"Some evenings after this, I was riding back from my brother's quarter-he was in the 15th, and was stationed about a mile from us-when I remarked the same dog I had seen before, trot up to a sentry who, with his legs crossed, was leaning against a wall. The man started, and began walking backwards and forwards on his beat. I recognised the dog by a large white streak on his side-all the rest of his coat being black.

"When I came up to the man, I saw it was Jokel Falck, and although I could not have said he was asleep, I strongly suspected that that was the fact.

"'You had better take care of yourself, my man,' said I. 'I have half a mind to have you relieved, and make a prisoner of you. I believe I should have found you asleep on your post, if that dog had not roused you.'

"Instead of looking penitent, as was usual on these occasions, I saw a half smile on the man's face, as he saluted me.

"'Whose dog is that?' I asked my servant, as I rode away.

"'Je ne sais pas mon, Colonel,' he answered, smiling too.

"On the same evening at mess, I heard one of the subalterns say to the officer who sat next him, 'It's a fact, I assure you, and they call him Mungo.'

"'That's a new name they've got for Schnapps, isn't it?' I said.

"'No, sir; it's the name of a dog,' replied the young man, laughing.

"'A black Newfoundland, with a large white streak on his flank?'

"'Yes, sir, I believe that is the description,' replied he, tittering still.

"'I have seen that dog two or three times,' said I. 'I saw him this evening-who does he belong to?'

"'Well, sir, that is a difficult question,' answered the lad; and I heard his companion say, 'To Old Nick, I should think.'

"'Do you mean to say you've really seen Mungo?' said somebody at the table.

"'If Mungo is a large Newfoundland-black, with a white streak on its side—I saw him just now. Who does he belong to?'

"By this time, the whole mess table was in a titter, with the exception of one old captain, a man who had been years in the regiment. He was of very humble extraction, and had risen by merit to his present position.

"'I believe Captain T. is better acquainted with Mungo than anybody present,' answered Major R., with a sneer. 'Perhaps he can tell you who he belongs to.'

"The laughter increased, and I saw there was some joke, but not understanding what it meant, I said to Captain G., 'Does the dog belong to Jokel Falck?'

"'No, sir,' he replied, 'the dog belongs to nobody now. He once belonged to an officer called Joseph Atveld.'

"'Belonging to this regiment?'

"'Yes, sir.'

"'He is dead, I suppose?'

"'Yes, sir, he is.'

"'And the dog has attached himself to the regiment?'

"'Yes, sir.'

"During this conversation, the suppressed laughter continued, and every eye was fixed on Captain T., who answered me shortly, but with the utmost gravity.

"'In fact,' said the major, contemptuously, 'according to Captain T., Mungo is the ghost of a deceased dog.'

"This announcement was received with shouts of laughter, in which I confess I joined, whilst Captain T. still retained an unmoved gravity.

"'It is easier to laugh at such a thing than to believe it, sir,' said he. '*I* believe it, because I know it.'

"I smiled, and turned the conversation.

"If anybody at the table except Captain T. had made such an assertion as this, I should have ridiculed them without mercy; but he was an old man, and from the circumstances I have mentioned regarding his origin, we were careful not to offend him; so no more was said about Mungo, and in the hurry of events that followed. I never thought of it again. We marched on to Brussels the next day; and after that, had enough to do till we went to Antwerp, where we were besieged by the French the following year.

"During the siege, I sometimes heard the name of Mungo again; and, one night, when I was visiting the guards and sentries as grand rounds, I caught a glimpse of him, and I felt sure that the man he was approaching when I observed him, had been asleep; but he was screened by an angle of the bastion, and by the time I turned the corner, he was moving about.

"This brought to my mind all I had heard about the dog; and as the circumstance was curious, in any point of view, I mentioned what I had seen to Captain T. the next day, saying, 'I saw your friend Mungo, last night.'

"'Did you, sir?' said he. 'It's a strange thing! No doubt, the man was asleep!'

"'But do you seriously mean to say, that you believe this to be a visionary dog, and not a dog of flesh and blood?'

"'I do, sir; I have been quizzed enough about it; and, once or twice, have nearly got into a quarrel, because people will persist in laughing at what they know nothing about; but as sure as that is a sword you hold in your hand, so sure is that dog a spectre, or ghost-if such a word is applicable to a fourfooted beast!'

"'But, it's impossible!' I said. 'What reason have you for such an extraordinary belief?'

"'Why, you know, sir, man-and-boy, I have been in the regiment all my life. I was born in it. My father was pay-serjeant of No. 3 company, when he died; and I have seen Mungo myself, perhaps twenty times, and known, positively, of others seeing him twice as many more.'

"'Very possibly; but that is no proof, that it is not some dog that has attached himself to the regiment.'

"'But I have seen and heard of the dog for fifty years, sir; and my father before me, had seen and heard of him as long!'

"'Well, certainly, that is extraordinary,—if you are sure of it, and that it's the same dog!'

"'It's a remarkable dog, sir. You won't see another like it with that large white streak on his flank. He won't let one of our sentries be found asleep, if he can help; unless, indeed, the fellow is drunk. He seems to have less care of drunkards, but Mungo has saved many a man from punishment. I was once, not a little indebted to him myself. My sister was married out of the regiment, and we had had a bit of a festivity, and drank rather too freely at the wedding, so that when I mounted guard that night—I wasn't to say, drunk, but my head was a little gone, or so; and I should have been caught nodding; but Mungo, knowing, I suppose, that I was not an habitual drunkard, woke me just in time.'

"'How did he wake you?' I asked.

"'I was roused by a short, sharp bark, that sounded close to my ears. I started up, and had just time to catch a glimpse of Mungo before he vanished!'

"'Is that the way he always wakes the men?'

"'So they say; and, as they wake, he disappears.'

"I recollected now, that on each occasion when I had observed the dog, I had, somehow, lost sight of him in an instant; and, my curiosity being awakened, I asked Captain T., if ours were the only men he took charge of, or, whether he showed the same attention to those of other regiments?

"'Only the 20th, sir; the tradition is, that after the battle of Fontenoy, a large black mastiff was found lying beside a dead officer. Although he had a dreadful wound from a sabre cut on his flank, and was much exhausted from loss of blood, he would not leave the body; and even after we buried it, he could not be enticed from the spot. The men, interested by the fidelity and attachment of the animal, bound up his wounds, and fed and tended him; and he became the dog of the regiment. It is said, that they had taught him to go his rounds before the guards and sentries were visited, and to wake any men that slept. How this may be, I cannot say; but he remained with the regiment till his death, and was buried with all the respect they could show him. Since that, he has shown his gratitude in the way I tell you, and of which you have seen some instances.'

"'I suppose the white streak is the mark of the sabre cut. I wonder you never fired at him.'

"'God forbid sir, I should do such a thing,' said Captain T., looking sharp round at me. 'It's said that a man did so once, and that he never had any luck afterwards; that may be a superstition, but I confess I wouldn't take a good deal to do it.'

"'If, as you believe, it's a spectre, it could not be hurt, you know; I imagine ghostly dogs are impervious to bullets.'

"'No doubt, sir; but I shouldn't like to try the experiment. Besides, it would be useless, as I am convinced already.'

"I pondered a good deal upon this conversation with the old captain. I had never for a moment entertained the idea that such a thing was possible. I should have as much expected to meet the minotaur or a flying dragon as a ghost of any sort, especially the ghost of a dog; but the evidence here was certainly startling. I had never observed anything like weakness and credulity about T.; moreover, he was a man of known courage, and very much respected in the regiment. In short, so much had his earnestness on the subject staggered me, that I resolved whenever it was my turn to visit the guards and sentries, that I would carry a pistol with me ready primed and loaded, in order to settle the question. If T. was right, there would be an interesting fact established, and no harm done; if, as I could not help suspecting, it was a cunning trick of the men, who had trained this dog to wake them, while they kept up the farce of the spectre, the animal would be well out of the way; since their reliance on him no doubt led them to give way to drowsiness when they would otherwise have struggled against it; indeed, though none of our men had been detected-thanks, perhaps, to Mungo-there had been so much negligence lately in the garrison that the general had issued very severe orders on the subject.

"However, I carried my pistol in vain; I did not happen to fall in with Mungo; and some time afterwards, on hearing the thing alluded to at the mess-table, I mentioned what I had done, adding, 'Mungo is too knowing, I fancy, to run the risk of getting a bullet in him.'

"'Well,' said Major R., 'I should like to have a shot at him, I confess. If I thought I had any chance of seeing him, I'd certainly try it; but I've never seen him at all.'

"'Your best chance,' said another, 'is when Jokel Falck is on duty. He is such a sleepy scoundrel, that the men say if it was not for Mungo he'd pass half his time in the guard house.'

"'If I could catch him I'd put an ounce of lead into him; that he may rely on.'

"'Into Jokel Falck, sir?' said one of the subs, laughing.

"'No, sir,' replied Major R.; 'into Mungo-and I'll do it, too.'

"'Better not, sir,' said Captain T., gravely; provoking thereby a general titter round the table.

"Shortly after this, as I was one night going to my quarter, I saw a mounted orderly ride in and call out a file of the guard to take a prisoner.

"'What's the matter?' I asked.

"'One of the sentries asleep on his post, sir; I believe it's Jokel Falck.'

"'It will be the last time, whoever it is,' I said; 'for the general is determined to shoot the next man that's caught.'

"'I should have thought Mungo had stood Jokel Falck's friend, so often that he'd never have allowed him to be caught,' said the adjutant. 'Mungo has neglected his duty.'

"'No, sir,' said the orderly, gravely. 'Mungo would have waked him, but Major R. shot at him.'

"'And killed him,' I said.

"The man made no answer, but touched his cap and rode away.

"I heard no more of the affair that night; but the next morning, at a very early hour, my servant woke me, saying that Major R. wished to speak to me. I desired he should be admitted, and the moment he entered the room, I saw by his countenance that something serious had occurred; of course, I thought the enemy had gained some unexpected advantage during the night, and sat up in bed inquiring eagerly what had happened.

"To my surprise he pulled out his pocket-handkerchief and burst into tears. He had married a native of Antwerp, and his wife was in the city at this time. The first thing that occurred to me was, that she had met with some accident, and I mentioned her name.

"'No, no,' he said; 'my son, my boy, my poor Fritz!'

"'You know that in our service, every officer first enters his regiment as a private soldier, and for a certain space of time does all the duties of that position. The major's son, Fritz, was thus in his noviciate. I concluded he had been killed by a stray shot, and for a minute or two I remained in this persuasion, the major's speech being choked by his sobs. The first words he uttered were —

"'Would to God I had taken Captain T.'s advice!'

"'About what?' I said. 'What has happened to Fritz?'

"'You know,' said he, 'yesterday I was field officer of the day; and when I was going my rounds last night, I happened to ask my orderly, who was assisting to put on my sash, what men we had told off for the guard. Amongst others, he named Jokel Falck, and remembering the conversation the other day at the mess table, I took one of my pistols out of the holster, and, after loading, put it in my pocket. I did not expect to see the dog, for I had never seen him; but as I had no doubt that the story of the spectre was some dodge of the men, I determined if ever I did, to have a shot at him. As I was going through the Place de Meyer, I fell in with the general, who joined me, and we rode on together, talking of the siege. I had forgotten all about the dog, but when we came to the rampart, above the Bastion du Matte, I suddenly saw exactly such an animal as the one described, trotting beneath us. I knew there must be a sentry immediately below where we rode, though I could not see him, and I had no doubt that the animal was making towards him; so without saying a word, I drew out my pistol and fired, at the same moment jumping off my horse, in order to look over the bastion, and get a sight of the man. Without comprehending what I was about, the general did the same, and there we saw the sentry lying on his face, fast asleep.'

"'And the body of the dog?' said I.

"'Nowhere to be seen,' he answered, 'and yet I must have hit him —I fired bang into him. The general says it must have been a delusion, for he was looking exactly in the same direction, and saw no dog at all-but I am certain I saw him, so did the orderly.'

"'But Fritz?' I said.

"'It was Fritz-Fritz was the sentry,' said the major, with a fresh burst of grief. The court-martial sits this morning, and my boy will be shot, unless interest can be made with the general to grant him a pardon.'

"I rose and drest myself immediately, but with little hope of success. Poor Fritz being the son of an officer, was against him rather than otherwise-it would have been considered an act of favouritism to spare him. He was shot; his poor mother died of a broken heart, and the major left the service immediately after the surrender of the city."

"And have you ever seen Mungo again?" said I.

"No," he replied; "but I have heard of others seeing him."

"And are you convinced that it was a spectre, and not a dog of flesh and blood?"

"I fancy I was then-but, of course, one can't believe —"

"Oh, no;" I rejoined; "Oh, no; never mind facts, if they don't fit into our theories."

The Old French Gentleman's Story

I spent the summer of fifty-six at Dieppe —a charming watering-place for those who can bear an exciting air, and are not very particular about what they eat. Dieppe, as travellers see it who are hurrying through to Paris, has a most unpromising aspect, with its muddy basins and third and fourth rate inns on the quays, but if you are not hastening from the packet to the train, which the great proportion of people do; you have only to pass up one of the short streets you will see *en face*, when you issue from the Custom-house, into which you have been introduced on landing, and you will find yourself on an esplanade of considerable extent, with a wide expanse of clear salt water before you, a fine terrace walk along the shore, and several newly erected hotels opposite the sea. Of course, there is an *etablissement* where the usual amusements are provided; the bathing is excellent, and the company numerous, for Dieppe is the favourite watering place of the fashionable world of Paris. The beauty of the place is greatly increased by a judicious suggestion of the Emperor's. I was told that when he and the Empress were there in '55, they complained of the absence of flowers on the esplanade; it was objected that none would grow there; however, he recommended them to try hollyhocks, china-asters, and poppies, the latter are the finest I ever saw, and the brilliant and varied masses of colour produce a very good effect. But they do not feed you well here; '*La Viande est longue à Dieppe*' as the Garçon of the Hôtel Royal urged when I objected to the meat which, on application of the knife fell into strips of pack-thread; the poultry is lean and bad; fish scarce, because it all goes to London or Paris, by contract, and everything dear. Nevertheless, Dieppe is a very nice place and the surrounding country is exceedingly pretty and picturesque.

Some members of the Jockey Club were in the Hôtel Royal, living very fast indeed. They all bore very aristocratic names and titles, but not the impress of high blood. How should they? Judging from what I saw, such a course of profligate self-indulgence, unredeemed, even by good breeding, must have effaced the stamp, if it ever was there. They inhabited a pavilion in the cour, and the luxurious repasts that we constantly saw served to them gave us an awful idea of the amount of their bill. They played at cards all day-the live long summer day! And only suspended this amusement when the garçons appeared with their trays loaded with expensive wines and high-seasoned dishes. One other amusement they had, which was no less an amusement to us-they had a drag —a regular English four-in-hand. The cour of the hotel was divided from the road by iron rails, with a large gate at each extremity for carriages, so that to an English whip, nothing would have been easier than to drive in at one of these gates, and round the sweep, and out at the other; but this the jockey club could never accomplish; when the gentlemen took the reins from the coachman, if they were in, they could not get out; and if they were out, they could not get in; so after a few ambitious attempts and ignominious failures, they submitted to the inglorious expediency of mounting and dismounting outside the gates. The French have certainly a remarkable incapacity for riding or driving, which is strange, as they are active men and have generally light figures. The Emperor is almost the only Frenchman I ever saw ride well; but he rides like an English gentleman.

There were many elegantly drest women, of all nations, at Dieppe, but there was one who particularly attracted my attention, and for whom, when I afterwards heard her story, I felt an extraordinary interest. This was the Countess Adeline de-Givry-Monjerac, at least so I will call her here. When I first saw her she was going down to bathe, attended by her maid, a grave elderly person, and I was so much struck by her appearance, that I took the first opportunity of enquiring her name. She was tall and very pale, with fine, straight features, and an expression of countenance at once noble and melancholy. Her figure was so good, and her bearing at once so graceful and dignified, that her unusual height did not strike you till you saw her standing beside other women. She was leaning on her maid's arm, and stooped a little, apparently from feebleness. Her attire was a peignoir of grey taffetas, lined with blue, and on her head she wore a simple capote of the same. Her age, I judged to be about forty.

She lodged in the Hôtel Royal, as I did also, but lived entirely in private; and we only saw her there as she went in and out. Later in the season, the Duchesse de B., and other persons, arrived from Paris, with whom she was acquainted, and I often observed her in conversation with them on the promenade; but her countenance never lost its expression of melancholy. However, I should have left Dieppe, ignorant of the singular circumstances I am about to relate, but for an accident.

There was a verandah in the court of the hotel, in which many of us preferred to breakfast, rather than in the salon; and the verandah not being very extensive, and the candidates numerous, there was often a little difficulty in securing a table. One morning, I had just laid my parasol on the only one I saw vacant, when the garçon warned me that it was already engaged by *ce monsieur*, indicating an old gentleman, who was standing with his back to me, in conversation with one of a sisterhood called *Soeurs de la Providence*, who was soliciting him to buy some of the lottery tickets she held in her hand; they were for the *Loterie de Bienfaisance*, the proceeds of which are devoted to charitable purposes. There are innumerable lotteries of this sort in France, authorized by the government; and they seem to me to be the substitute for our magnificent private charities in England, for very large sums are collected. The tickets only cost a franc. I believe the *tirage* is conducted with perfect fairness; and people thus subscribe a franc for the poor, with the agreeable, but very remote, chance of being repaid, *même ici bas*, a hundred thousand-fold.

The old gentleman turned his head on hearing my conversation with the waiter; and, begging I would not derange myself on his account, desired that I might have the table. Grateful for such an unusual exertion of politeness-for the politeness of the modern French gentleman does not include the smallest modicum of self-sacrifice —I modestly declined, and said, "I would wait." He answered, "by no means." And while we were engaged in this amicable contest, the waiter brought his breakfast, and placed it on the table; seeing which, he proposed, that as he was denied the pleasure of making way for me, I should have my coffee placed on the other side, and we should breakfast together; an offer which I gladly accepted.

He was a pleasant, garrulous, old gentleman. Monsieur de Vennacour was his name, *proprietaire à Paris*, and he told me how he had lost his fortune by the revolutions, and how he lived now in a *petit apartment* in the *Rue des Ecuries d'Anjou*, and belonged to a coterie of old ladies and gentlemen like himself, who had a *petit whisk* every night during the winter. While we were talking, the Countess passed us on her way to the bath; and, happening to catch her eye as she crossed the court, he bowed to her; whereupon I asked him if he knew her?

"A little," he said; "but I knew her husband well; and her mother's hotel was next to that my family formerly inhabited. She was a beautiful woman, Madame de Lignerolles."

"Then, she is dead?" said I.

"No," he replied. "She has retired from the world, —she is in a convent. C'est une histoire bien triste celle de Madame de Lignerolles et sa fille, et aussi bien etrange!"

"If it is not a secret, perhaps you will tell it to me?" said I; for I saw that my new acquaintance desired nothing better. He was a famous raconteur; and I wish I could tell the story in English as well, and as dramatically, as he told it to me in French; however, I'll repeat it as faithfully as I can.

"Madame de Lignerolles née Hermione de Givry, was married early to the Marquis de Lignerolles, without any particular *penchant* for or against the union. The Marquis was a great deal older than herself, but it was considered a good match, for he was very rich, and his genealogy was unexceptionable. Not more so, however, than the young lady's; for the de Givry's heraldic tree had apparently sprung from an acorn floated to the west by Deucalion himself. At the period of Hermione's marriage her father, mother, and two brothers, older than herself, still lived. Her father, the Comte de Givry had been a younger son, and had inherited the fortune on the death of his elder brother who was killed in a duel the day before he was to have been married to a woman he passionately loved. He died by the hand of one of his most intimate friends, with whom he had never had a word of difference before, and the subject of quarrel was a peacock! But it was always remarked by the world, that the eldest scions of the house of Givry were singularly unfortunate; they seldom prospered in their loves, and if they did, they were sure to die before their hopes were realised. People in general called it *a destiny*; others whispered that it was a curse; but the family laughed contemptuously if any one presumed to hint such a thing in their presence, and asserted that it was merely *le hazard*; and as the world in these days is very much disposed to believe in *le hazard*, few persons sought to penetrate further into the cause of these misadventures. However, Hermione's elder brother, Etienne, did not escape his *mauvais destin*; the lady he was engaged to marry was seized with the smallpox, and, from being a pretty person, became a very ugly one. During her illness, he had sworn nothing should break his engagement, and accordingly, disfigured as she was, he married her; but he had better, for both their sakes, have left it alone. He was disgusted and she was jealous; they parted within a month after the wedding, and he was soon after killed by a fall from his horse in the Bois de Boulogne, and died, leaving no issue. Upon his decease, the second son, Armande, now the heir, was recalled from Prussia, whither he had gone with his regiment, but they were on the eve of a battle, and it was not consistent with his honour to leave till it was over. He was the first officer that fell in the fight, and thus the hopes of the ancient family of Givry became centered in the offspring of Hermione. But, Adeline, the fair object of my admiration, was the sole fruit of the marriage, and great were the lamentations of the old Count and Countess that the continuation of this noble stock rested on so frail a tenure, for the child was exceedingly delicate; she outgrew her strength, and for some years was supposed to be *poitrinaire*. But, either, thanks to the wonderful care that was bestowed upon her, or to an inherent good constitution, she survived this trying period and grew up to marriageable years, rewarding all the solicitude of her family by her charms and amiability. She was not so beautiful as her mother had been-and even was still-but she was quite sufficiently handsome; and there was so much grace in her movements and her manners, and she had such a noble and pure expression of countenance —a true indication of her character-that Adeline de Lignerolle's perfections were universally admitted by the men, and scarcely denied by the women, insomuch, that these attractions, added to her lineage and fortune, caused her to be looked upon as one of the most desirable matches in the kingdom.

"Her father, the old Marquis de Lignerolles-Givry—for he was constrained to adopt the latter name-had died previous to this period; and as her grandfather Monsieur de Givry undertook the affair of her marriage, numerous were the propositions he privately received, and frequent the closettings and consultations on the subject. In these cases, the more people have, the more they require; and as Adeline had better blood, and more money, than most people, the family exigence in these respects was considerable, and the difficulties that lay in the way of procuring a suitable alliance, manifold.

"She had reached the age of seventeen, and this important point was still unsettled, when she and her mother went to visit a relative of Madame de Lignerolles, who was united to a Portuguese nobleman. On her marriage, she had followed her husband to his own country; but he was now on a mission to the French court; and the Paris season being over, they had taken a château on the Loire, for the summer months. There were other young people in the house, and all sorts of amusements going on, which no one seemed to enjoy, at first, more than Adeline de Givry; but, at the end of a fortnight, a change began to be observable in her spirits and demeanour, which did not escape the observation of her young companions; and by their means awakened the attention of Madame de Saldanha, their hostess; who hinted to her cousin, Madame de Lignerolles, that Adeline was falling in love with the young Count de la Cruz; at least, such was the opinion of her own daughter, Isabella; adding, that if so abnormal a circumstance, as a young lady choosing her own husband *was* to happen, she could not have fixed on a more desirable individual than Rodriguez de la Cruz, —a man unexceptionable in person, mind, and manners whose genealogy might vie with that of the De Givry's themselves; and whose name was associated with distinguished deeds of arms during the Holy Wars.

"But this indulgent view of the case was not shared by Madame de Lignerolles. She seemed exceedingly surprised and incredulous; but when the other insisted on the probability of such a result, since the two young people had been residing for six weeks under the same roof; and pointed out to the lady that the assiduous attentions paid by De la Cruz to herself were, doubtless, not without an object, suggesting that that object was to gain her interest in his favour, she evinced so much displeasure and indignation, that Madame de Saldanha apologized and gave up the point, saying, she was very likely mistaken, and that it was a mere fancy of Isabella's.

"Nevertheless, these suspicions were perfectly well founded. De la Cruz was waiting for his father's consent to make his proposals in form; and this consent was only delayed till the old gentleman had time to come to Paris and make the needful inquiries regarding fortune and family; about which, he considered himself entitled to be quite as particular as the De Givry's.

"It was remarked that, from this time, Madame de Lignerolles observed her daughter with a jealous eye, and sought every means of keeping her away from the young Portuguese; added to which, as it afterwards appeared, she severely reproved Adeline for what she called the levity of her conduct.

"Moreover, she hastened her departure; and in a few days after the conversation with Madama de Saldanha, took her leave; alleging, that her presence was required by her father, in Paris. To Paris, however, she did not immediately go. There was in Brittany an ancient château belonging to the family, which, for some reason or other, they very rarely visited; it was supposed, because they possessed others more agreeable. At all events, whatever might be the cause, it was known that the old count had a mortal aversion to this residence, insomuch, that his daughter had never been there since her infancy; when something very unpleasant was reported to have happened to her mother's eldest brother shortly before his death. Thither, however, they now travelled with all speed, accompanied only by two maids and a man.

"Madame de Lignerolles was a person, in whom the maternal instinct had never been largely developed. She was even, still, at eight-and-thirty, a beautiful woman; and it was generally suspected, that she did not feel at all delighted at having this tall, handsome daughter, to proclaim her age; and, perhaps shortly, make her a grandmother. But, her manner to Adeline-usually, more indifferent than harsh-now assumed a new character; she seemed engrossed with her own thoughts; was cold and constrained; spoke little; and when she did, it was with a gravity truly portentous.

"They were not unexpected at Château Noir-for such was the ominous name of the old castle, which frowned upon them in the gloom of a dusky November evening; but instead of the liveried servants, by whom they were accustomed to be greeted, an elderly housekeeper, a concierge, and a few rustic menials, appeared to be its only inhabitants. However, they had done their best to make ready for this visit; fires were lighted, and dinner was prepared and served, accompanied by plenty of apologies for its not being better.

"The evening passed in silence; they were tired, and went early to bed. The next two days, Mdme. de Lignerolles kept her room, and Adeline strolled about the neglected grounds, occupied with her own thoughts of the future, not without wondering a little at her mother's mysterious behaviour. On the third day, she was summoned to the presence of Mdme. de Lignerolles, who received and bade her be seated, with the same significant solemnity, and then proceeded to inform her that she had a most painful secret to communicate —a secret that had long prest upon her conscience, but which she could never find resolution to disclose; that lately, however, her confessor had so strongly urged her to perform this act of duty, that, with the greatest reluctance, she had resolved to obey his injunctions-her doing so having become more imperative from the fact of Adeline's having arrived at marriageable years, as in the event of any alliance presenting itself, honour would constrain her to speak. The dreadful secret was, that Adeline was not her child; that the nurse who had had the charge of her infancy, confessed on her death-bed, that she had substituted her own infant for the countess's, that the latter had subsequently died, but that she could not leave the world in peace without avowing her crime.

"'I did not believe her,' said Mdme. de Lignerolles, 'but she reminded me that my child had a mole under the left breast, which you, Adeline, have not. This cruel change was effected during our absence from France. Shortly after my confinement, I was ordered to spend the winter in Italy, and the child was left to the care of my father and mother, who by that time had nearly lost her eye-sight. To this circumstance, and the little notice men usually take of infants, the woman trusted to escape detection. Of course, I could not discern the difference between the child I had left and the one I found. I had no suspicion; and whatever alterations I remarked, I attributed to the lapse of time-though I must own that maternal instinct offered a strong confirmation of the nurse's confession. While I believed you my own offspring, I had none of those tender yearnings which I have heard other women speak of, and I often reproached myself for the want of them. However, I endeavoured to do my duty by you, and no pains or expense were spared on your education, which was already nearly completed, when I became acquainted with this dreadful secret, of which, when the nurse died, I was the sole possessor. But, aware of the intense grief such a disclosure would occasion my husband, who was then in exceedingly bad health, I determined during his lifetime to preserve silence. After his death, I ought to have exerted courage to speak; but my mother adored you-it would have killed her. She is now gone, and there is only your grandfather left. I well know the suffering it will cause him, and, believe me, I feel for *you* —but my duty is plain. You will be amply provided for—' but ere the sentence could be finished, Adeline, who had sat like a statue, listening to this harangue, with wondering eyes and open lips, suddenly rose and rushed out of the room. That she was not Mdme. de Lignerolles' daughter caused her little grief, nor was she of an age very highly to appreciate the position and splendours she was losing; but she thought of her grandfather, whom she really loved; she thought of De la Cruz, and her heart filled with anguish.

"She was not pursued to her retreat; the whole day she kept her chamber, and Mdme. de Lignerolles kept hers. On the following morning, a note was handed to her from Mdme. de L., announcing that she was starting for Paris to communicate this distressing intelligence to M. de Givry; and desiring Adeline to remain where she was, under the care of Mdme. Vertot, the housekeeper, till she received further directions; assuring her, at the same time, that everything should be done for her happiness and welfare, and, in due time, a suitable *parti* be provided for her."

Just as Monsieur de Venacour reached this point of his story, Madame de Montjerac returned from bathing, and if I looked at her with interest before, it may be well imagined how much more she inspired now.

"How extraordinary!" I said, as my eyes rested on her noble countenance and majestic figure, "that that distinguished-looking woman is really the daughter of a good-for-nothing servant; and yet I should have said, if ever there was a person who bore the unmistakeable impress of aristocracy, it is she."

He nodded his head, and significantly lifting his fore-finger to the side of his nose, said "Ecoutez!" and forthwith proceeded with his narration as follows.

"On Madam de Lignerolle's arrival in Paris, she sent for her father, threw herself at his feet, and with tears and lamentations, disclosed this dreadful secret, which, she said, had been making the misery of her life for the last two years; but whatever distress it occasioned her, it was quite evident that that of Monsieur de Givry was much more severe. He was wounded on all sides; his pride, his love of lineage, his personal affection for Adeline, and his horror of the notoriety such an extraordinary event must naturally acquire. So powerful were the two last sentiments, that for a moment he even entertained the idea of accepting Adeline as the heiress of Givry, and concealing the whole affair from her and every body else; but to this proposition his daughter objected that the poor girl was already in possession of the truth, and that it was impossible to make her a party to such a deception.

"'Then,' said Monsieur de Givry, 'she must die! There is no other expedient.'

"'Mais, non, mon pere!' cried Hermione, starting from her seat, evidently taken quite aback by this unexpected proposition.

"De Givry waved his hand with a melancholy smile; 'Enfant!' he said. 'Do you think I intend to become an assassin? God forbid!' And then he explained that he did not mean a real but a fictitious death, for which purpose she must be removed to a foreign country, under the pretence of the re-appearance of pulmonary symptoms; that a husband must be found for her who would bind himself to leave France for ever, and to keep this secret, under pain of forfeiting the very handsome allowance he proposed to make them; for the safe conduct of which part of the business, it would be necessary to confide their unhappy circumstances to the family physician and lawyer. In the meantime, as these arrangements could not be made in a day, it was decided that Adeline should remain where she was till all was ready for their completion.

"'I shall take her out of the country myself,' he said, 'and you must accompany us. Every consideration must be shown her; she is the victim, and not the criminal.'

"In the course of this conversation, as may be imagined, Monsieur de Givry more than once lamented the extinction of his race; his daughter, however, on that point, offered him some consolation, by suggesting that she was still a young woman, and that for her father's sake, although she had never intended to marry again, she would consent to do so provided she could meet with an unobjectionable *parti*.

"Shortly after this melancholy disclosure, De la Cruz arrived with his father in Paris; where they were so well received by Madame de Lignerolles, that the old gentleman, fascinated by her beauty and manners, expressed his surprise that his son had not fallen in love with the mother, instead of the daughter. However, at his son's desire, he made formal propositions for the young lady's hand; which, to the surprise of the young man, Monsieur de Livry said, was already promised; adding, however, that his granddaughter's state of health would, probably, retard the union; the physicians having discovered that the seeds of consumption were beginning to develope themselves in her constitution, and, consequently, recommended her removal to a warmer climate.

"In the meanwhile, the poor young girl was pining alone in the dreary, old château, with no companion but her own maid,—receiving no intelligence, and ignorant of her future fate. All she knew was, that she never could be the wife of Rodriguez de la Cruz. She supposed, that when he made his proposals, he would be informed of the circumstances above related, and that she should never hear more of him. But, in this, she was mistaken. About three weeks after her mother had left her, a letter from him arrived, saying, that he had succeeded in discovering where she was, and that he had lost no time in writing to inform her of the ill fortune that had attended his proposals; adding, that if her sentiments continued unchanged, he would come to Château Noir, accompanied by his own chaplain, who would unite them; after which, he had no doubt, it would be easy to obtain her grandfather's forgiveness; he, probably, having only refused his consent because he was trammelled by a prior engagement.

"But this letter was addressed to Mademoiselle de Lignerolles; and it was evident, from the whole tenour of it, that the writer knew nothing of the change in her fortunes. Honour forbad her to take advantage of this ignorance; but the struggle threw her into agonies of grief. She passed a miserable day, and retired early to bed; where she might indulge her tears, and avoid the curious eyes of her maid, who was greatly perplexed at these unusual proceedings. Sleep was far from her eyes, and her mind was busy, framing the answer she had to write on the following day to De la Cruz, when she heard a knock at her chamber door. 'Come in,' she said; not doubting that it was her maid, or Madame Vertot. Immediately, she heard the handle turned, and she saw in a mirror that was opposite, the door open, and a miserable, haggard-looking woman enter. She was attired in rags, and she led by the hand two naked children. They approached the foot of the bed, and the woman held out a letter, as if she wished Adeline to take it, which she made an effort to do; but a sudden horror seized her, and she uttered a scream which roused her maid who slept in the adjoining apartment. She was found insensible; but the usual applications restored her; and, without telling what had happened, she requested the servant to pass the rest of the night in her room. The next day, she felt very poorly in consequence of this horrid vision; but she wrote to De la Cruz such a letter, as she felt her altered circumstances demanded. She could not bring herself to avow that she was the daughter of Robertine Collet; but sent him, simply, a cold, haughty refusal, which precluded all possibility of any further advances. The next day, she changed her room, and she saw no more of the frightful apparition.

"She had done her duty to De la Cruz, but she was miserable; and when, shortly afterwards, her grandfather arrived, accompanied by Dr. Pecher, the family physician, they found her exceedingly ill, and confined to her bed. This Dr. Pecher was a clever and worthy man; and having been necessarily made the confidant of the painful secret, it had been privately arranged between him and Monsieur de Givry, that he should marry the girl; and that they should, thereupon, quit the country, —Monsieur de G. making ample provision for their future maintenance.

"But the main thing needful, was to restore her to health; and in the course of his attendance on her, he learnt from her maid how she had been first attacked; and then elicited from herself, the cause of her alarm. Of course, he looked upon the vision as an illusion; in short, the premonitory symptoms of her illness, —and mentioned it in that light, to Monsieur de Givry. But to his surprise, Monsieur de G. took a different view of the matter; and hastening to Adeline's room, he made her repeat to him the exact description of what she had seen; after which, he started immediately for Paris, without explaining the motive of this sudden departure.

"On his arrival, he presented himself before his daughter, and taxed her with having deceived him; what her motive could be he was unable to imagine; he supposed it to be pecuniary, and that she did not wish to part with the large portion to be paid to Adeline on her marriage; but he believed that the traditionary apparition of his family would not have appeared to any one who was not a member of it; and that therefore the girl, who had accurately described the appearance of these figures, of which the young people were always kept in entire ignorance, must be actually his granddaughter.

"Madame de Lignerolles persisted in her story, and all she could be brought to own was, that it was possible, the woman, Collett, had deceived her. Strong in his own opinion, Monsieur de Givry returned to Château Noir, Dr. Pecher having recommended the young lady's removal; and after writing his daughter a very urgent and serious letter, he started on a tour of a few weeks, with Adeline, for the recovery of her health.

"No answer reached him for some time, but at the end of a month, he received one, acknowledging the cruel deception she had practiced, alleging as her excuse, an ardent passion for Rodriguez de la Cruz; and the wish to detach him from Adeline, and marry him herself. But she had failed, and he was on the point of marriage with a lady selected for him by his father. The letter concluded by the announcement, that she was about to retire to a convent where she should, in due time, take the veil.

"Monseiur de Givry assumed this to be a mere ebullition of shame and disappointment; but she kept her word. Mademoiselle de Lignerolles, some years later, married the Baron de Montjerac, from whom, said Monsieur de Venacour, I heard the story. By him she had two sons; but the constant apprehension that in the eldest will be fulfilled the *mauvais destin* entailed on the heirs of Givry, preys, it is said, on her mind and health, and is the cause of the expression of melancholy for which her fine countenance is so remarkable.

"Some centuries earlier, when power was irresponsible, Count Armand de Givry, a cruel and oppressive lord of the soil, who then inhabited Château Noir, had put to death one of his serfs, and turned his wife and two children out of doors in inclement weather, forbidding any of his tenants to shelter or assist them. The children were without clothes, and the three poor creatures perished from cold and starvation, but leaving behind them a terrible retribution, in the form of a curse pronounced by the wretched woman's lips in her dying agonies, which, strange to say, seems to have been pretty literally fulfilled.

"When they were nearly at the last extremity, some good Christian had had the courage to write a pathetic letter for her, which, however, it was necessary she should deliver herself, as no one else durst do it. She watched her opportunity; concealed herself in the park, and waylaid the Count as he returned one day from shooting. But instead of taking the letter, he set his dogs upon her, who would have torn her to pieces, but for the courageous interference of one of his followers.

"The curse ran, that never should the heir of Givry prosper till one of them took the letter; and that the last scion of the house should *Renier le croix et se vouer à l'Enfer*.

"Since that, it was said that, no eldest son or daughter of the house of Givry had lived and prospered, whilst the letter, in some way or other had been offered to every one of them; but as the cadets of the family lived and married and prospered like other people, they did not choose to believe in the story; at least, whatever their secret thoughts on the subject may have been, they publicly threw ridicule on the tradition, whenever it was alluded to; but Monsieur de Givry had sufficient faith in it to believe, that if Adeline had been the daughter of Robertine Collet, she would never have been visited by the ghost of Madeleine Dogue and her children."

The Swiss Lady's Story

"It was not I," said Madame de Geirsteche; "it was my mother who saw the apparition you have heard of; but I can tell you all the particulars of the story if you have patience to listen to it."

"You would be conferring a great favour," I said; "from what I have heard of the circumstance, I am already much interested."

We were in the steamboat that plies between Vevay and Geneva when this conversation occurred, and as there could not be a more convenient opportunity of hearing the narration, we retired from the crowd of travellers that thronged the deck, and Madame de G. began as follows.

"My husband's father, the elder Monsieur Geirsteche, was acquainted with two young men named Zwengler. He was at school and at college with them, and their intimacy continued after their education was finished. When one was fourteen and the other ten, they had the misfortune to lose both their parents by an accident. They were crossing the Alps, when by the fall of an avalanche their carriage was overturned down a precipice, and they and their servants perished.

"The Zwenglers were people of good family but small fortune; and as they had always lived fully up to what they had, their property, when it came to be divided between their four children, for they had two daughters besides the sons I have named, afforded but an inadequate portion to each; but this misfortune was mitigated by their rich relations—a wealthy uncle adopted the boys, and an equally wealthy aunt took the girls. This was but just, for they had both been enriched by what ought to have been the inheritance of the other sister, the mother of these children, who, having married Monsieur Zwengler contrary to the wishes of her parents, was cut off with a shilling. This uncle and aunt had never married, for their father objected to every match that was proposed, as not sufficiently advantageous; whilst the brother and sister, taking warning by the fate of Madame Zwengler, preferred living single to the risk of incurring the same penalty. The daughters having good fortunes married early, and I believe did well enough; it is on the history of the sons that my story turns.

"As I mentioned, they were at the same school with my husband's father when the catastrophe happened to their parents, and he remembered afterwards the different manner in which the news had affected them; Alfred's grief was apparently stormy and violent; that of the other was less demonstrative, but more genuine. Alfred, in short, was secretly elated at the independence he expected would be the consequence of this sudden bereavement; and he lost no time in assuming over Louis the importance and authority of an elder brother. Louis was an enthusiastic, warm-hearted, and imaginative child, too young to appreciate his loss in a worldly point of view, but mourning his parents-especially his mother-sincerely.

"Alfred's hopes of independence were considerably abated, when he found himself under the guardianship of Mr. Altorf, his uncle, a proud, pompous, tenacious, arbitrary man; on the other hand, he was somewhat consoled by the expectation of becoming the heir to his large fortune, the magnitude of which he had frequently heard descanted on by his parents. He soon discovered, too, that as the heir expectant he had acquired an importance that he had never enjoyed before; and in order to make sure of these advantages, he neglected no means of recommending himself to the old gentleman, insomuch, that Mr. Altorf, being very fond of the study of chemistry, Alfred affected great delight in the same pursuit, sacrificing his own inclinations to shut himself up in his uncle's laboratory, with crucibles and chemicals that he often wished might be consumed in the furnace they employed. Louis, the while, pursued his studies, thoughtless of the future as young people usually are; but as he advanced in age, he began to exhibit symptoms of a failing constitution, and as the law for which his uncle designed him required more study than was compatible with health, he was allowed to follow his inclination and become a soldier. With this view, he was sent to Paris, and committed to the surveillance of a friend of his uncle there, who was in the French service.

"No profession being proposed for Alfred, he lived on with his uncle, confirmed in the belief that though his brother, if he survived, would be remembered in the old man's will, he himself should inherit the bulk of the property. It was a weary life to him, shut up half the day in the laboratory, that he detested, in constant association with an uncongenial companion. Moreover, up to the period of his being of age, he was kept almost entirely without money, and was excluded from all the pleasures suitable to his years. When he attained his majority, he became possessed of the small patrimony that devolved on him as the eldest son of his father, and was enabled to make himself some amends for the privations he had previously submitted to. Not that he threw off his uncle's authority, or became openly less submissive and conformable; but secretly he contrived to procure himself many relaxations and enjoyments, from which he had before been shut out; and in the attaining and purchasing these pleasures he freely squandered all the proceeds of his inheritance, reckoning securely on the future being well provided for.

"His uncle inhabited a villa outside of Geneva, on the road to Ferney, and seldom came into the town, except when he visited his banker. His chemicals and other articles, Alfred usually purchased, and he had made acquaintance with several young men, whose society and amusements he availed himself of these opportunities to enjoy. One frosty day in December, he was strolling arm in arm with some of these youths, when, on turning a corner, he unexpectedly saw sailing down the street before them, the massive figure of his uncle, attired in his best chocolate suit, his hair powdered, and a long pigtail hanging down his back. The air of conscious importance and pomposity with which he strode along, amused these gay companions, and they were diverting themselves at the old gentleman's expense, when his foot slipped on a slide, and he fell down. This was irresistible; and they all burst into a simultaneous shout of laughter. A passer by immediately assisted him to rise; and as he did so, he turned round to see from whence the merriment proceeded-perhaps he had recognised his nephew's voice-at all events, Alfred felt sure he *saw*, if he did not *hear*, and thought it prudent to apologise for his ill-timed hilarity, which he sought to excuse by alleging that he had not at first been aware who it was that had fallen. Mr. Altorf looked stern; but as he said nothing, and never alluded to the subject again, Alfred congratulated himself at having got off so well, and endeavoured to efface any unpleasant impression that might remain by extra attentions and compliances.

"Everything went on as usual till the following year, when one morning the old gentleman was found dead in his bed, and the medical men pronounced that he had expired in a fit of apoplexy.

"When the will-which was dated several years back-came to be read, it was found that after two trifling legacies, and five thousand pounds to Louis, the whole estate was bequeathed to Alfred, whose breast dilated with joy, as the words fell upon his ear, although it was no more than he was prepared for; but the first flush of triumph had not subsided, when the lawyer arrested the incipient congratulations of the company, by saying, 'Here is a codicil, I see, dated the fourteenth of December, last year.'

"The company resumed their seats, and a cold chill crept through Alfred's veins, as the reader proceeded as follows: —

"'I hereby revoke the bequest hereabove made to my nephew Alfred Zwengler, and I give and bequeath the whole of my estates, real and personal, to my nephew, Louis Zwengler. To my nephew, Alfred Zwengler, I give and bequeath my bust, which stands on the hall table. It is accounted a good likeness, and when I am gone, it will serve to keep him merry. May he have many a hearty laugh at it-on the wrong side of his mouth.'

"The auditors looked confounded on hearing this extraordinary paragraph, but Alfred understood it too well.

"It is unnecessary to dwell upon his feelings; a quarter of an hour ago he was one of the richest men of his canton-now there were not many poorer in all Switzerland than Alfred Zwengler. He had awakened from his long dream of wealth and importance, and habits of expense, to poverty and utter insignificance; while Louis, whom he had always despised-Louis, over whom he had domineered, and assumed the airs of an elder brother and a great man, had leapt into his shoes at one bound, and left him grovelling in the mud. How he hated him.

"But he might die; what letters they had had from Paris reported him very sickly; he might be killed in battle, for Europe was full of wars in those days; but he might do neither; and at all events, in the meantime what was Alfred to do? A thousand wild and desperate schemes passed through his brain for bettering his situation, but none seemed practicable. The sole remnant of the property he had inherited from his father, that still remained in his possession, was a house in Geneva, called L'Hôtel Dupont, that he had mortgaged to nearly its full value, intending at his uncle's death, to pay the money and redeem it. It had been let, but was now empty and under repair, and the creditors talked of selling it to pay themselves. But Alfred induced them to wait, by giving out that as soon as his brother understood his situation, he would advance the necessary sum to relieve him. Perhaps he really entertained this expectation, but he had no precise right to do so, for he had never given Louis a crown piece, though the latter had suffered much more from his uncle's parsimony than he had, having inherited nothing whatever from his parents. However, Alfred wrote to Louis, dating his letter from that house, dilating on his difficulties, and the hardness of his fate, and hinting that, had he come into possession of his uncle's fortune, as he had every right to expect he should, how he should have felt it his duty to act towards an only brother.

"He received no answer to this appeal; and, at first, he drew very unfavourable conclusions from his brother's silence; but, as time went on, and Louis neither appeared to take possession of his inheritance, nor wrote to account for his absence, hope began once more to dawn in the horizon; the brighter, that no letters whatever arrived from him; even the lawyers who had applied for instructions, received no answer. The last letter his uncle had had from him, had mentioned the probability of his joining the Republican forces in the south, if his health permitted him to do so. Altogether, there certainly were grounds for anxiety or hope, as it might be; I need not say which it was on this occasion. Rumours of bloody battles, too, prevailed, in which many had fallen. Even the creditors were content to wait, not being inclined to push to extremity a debtor, who might be on the verge of prosperity, for it was not likely that Louis would make a will; and it was even possible that he might have died before his uncle. In either case, Alfred was the undoubted heir; and, accordingly, he began once more to taste some of the sweets of fortune;—hats were doffed, hands were held out to him, and one or two sanguine spirits went so far as to offer loans of small sums and temporary accommodation.

"At length, affairs being in this state of uncertainty, the lawyers thought it necessary to investigate the matter, and endeavour to ascertain what was become of the heir. Measures were accordingly taken, which evidently kept Alfred in a violent state of agitation; but the result, apparently, made him amends for all he had suffered. It was proved that Louis, with his military friend, had joined the Republican forces in the south, but was supposed to have perished in an encounter with the Chouans; nobody could swear to having seen him dead; but, as the Republicans had been surprised and fallen into an ambush, they had been obliged to retreat, leaving their dead upon the field.

"This being the case, the property was given up to Alfred; a portion being sequestered, in order that it might accumulate for a certain number of years, for the purpose of refunding the original heir, should he-contrary to all expectation-reappear. If not, at the expiration of that term, the sequestrated portion would be released.

"Alfred Zwengler was now at the summit of his wishes; and one might have thought, would have felt the more intense satisfaction, in the possession of his wealth, from the narrow escape he had had of losing it; but this did not seem to be the case. He had, formerly, been very fond of society, though he had few opportunities of entering into it; but when he had, nobody enjoyed it more. Now, he did not shun mankind; on the contrary, he sought their company; but he was moody, silent, and apparently unhappy. People said, that he lived in constant fear of his brother's turning up again and reclaiming his inheritance. It might be so; nobody knew the cause of the change in him, for he was uncommunicative, even to his nearest acquaintance.

"One thing, that gave colour to this supposition was, that he evidently disliked to hear Louis named; and whenever he was alluded to, he invariably asserted that he did not believe he was dead, and that he expected every day to see him come back. After saying this, it was observed that, he would turn deathly pale,—rising from his chair, and walking about the room in manifest agitation.

"Preferring the town to the country, Mr. Zwengler had declared his intention of residing in his own house, which had lately been repaired under his special directions, and fitted up with all the appliances of comfort and elegance; but he was scarcely settled there before he took a sudden and unaccountable dislike to it, and offered it for sale. As it was an excellent property, Mr. Geirsteche, my husband's father bought it; and Mr. Zwengler purchased another house and removed his furniture thither.

"Mr. Geirsteche had no intention of living in the house; he bought it as an investment; for being situated in one of the best streets of the city, it was sure to let well; and accordingly it was not long before he found an eligible tenent in Mr. Bautte, an eminent watchmaker of Geneva, who furnished it handsomely. He was very rich, and wanted it for his family, who expressed themselves delighted with their new residence. Nevertheless, they had not been in it three months before they expressed a desire to live in the environs of the city rather than in it. As Mr. Bautte had taken a long lease of the house, he put up a ticket announcing that it was to be let. A gentleman from Lucerne, named Maurice, who had just married his sister's governess, and wished therefore to reside at a distance from his family, took it for three years, with the option of keeping it on for whatever term he pleased at the end of that period. He gave directions for the furnishing, and when it was ready, they came to Geneva and took up their abode in their new house. At the end of a year, they applied to Mr. Bautte for permission to sub-let the house. There was no such provision in the agreement, and Mr. Bautte at first, we were told, objected, but consented after an interview with Mr. Maurice. But these frequent removals had begun to draw observation, and it began to be rumoured that there was something objectionable about the Hôtel du Pont. The common people whispered that it was haunted; some said it was infested with rats; others that it was ill drained; in short, it got a bad reputation, and nobody was willing to take it. Mr. Maurice and his wife, who were gone to Paris for a few months, and had not yet removed their furniture, being informed of this, advertised it to be let furnished. So many strangers come to Geneva, that there is no want of tenants for good furnished houses, and it was soon engaged by a French family from Dijon. They took it for a year, but at the end of that time they left it for a residence much inferior in every respect, and yet more expensive; the rent Mr. Maurice asked being very moderate.

"I don't know who were the next tenants, but family after family took the house, for it was a very attractive one, but nobody lived in it long. When Mr. Maurice's three years had expired, Mr. Bautte bought his furniture, and continued to let the house furnished. He would have been glad to sell his lease, which was for thirty years, but nobody was inclined to buy it.

"I now, said Madame de G. come to that part of the story that concerns my mother. I have frequently heard the story from her own lips, and nothing made her so angry as to see people listen to it with incredulity. My grandfather, Mr. Colman, was, as you are aware, much given to the pursuit of literature, and as that is one that seldom brings wealth, his means were somewhat restricted, although he had a small independance of his own. He had three daughters and two sons, and when his family had outgrown their childhood, and my mother, who was the eldest, had attained the age of seventeen, they came to Geneva for the sake of giving the young people some advantages of education that he could not afford them in England; besides there was a good deal of literary society to be had here then, and the place was cheaper than it is now.

"Having no acquaintance, they applied on their arrival to an agent, who offered them several houses and L'Hôtel du Pont amongst the number. At first they were about to decline it as a residence beyond their means; but when the rent was named, they took it immediately. It was so far the best house they had seen, and the cheapest, that when the agreement was signed, they expressed their surprise to the agent, at what appeared the unreasonable demands of the other proprietors.

"'Why, this house is particularly situated, sir,' said the agent. 'The gentleman who furnished it was obliged to leave Geneva almost immediately after he had settled himself here; and he being absent, and caring more for a good tenant than a high rent, we don't stand out for a price as people must do when they look to make money by a house.'

"Mr. Colman congratulated himself on his good luck in finding such a liberal proprietor, and in a few days he and his family were comfortably established in the Hôtel du Pont. The only difficulty they had found was in procuring servants. They had one English maid with them, and, at last, they succeeded in getting two girls as cook and housemaid. The latter was a German, who had been brought there by a family who had gone on to Italy; and the former was a Frenchwoman, who had married a gentleman's valet, and had followed him from Paris to Geneva.

"As soon as everything was arranged, they resumed their usual habits-one of which was, that for an hour or two before they went to bed the father read aloud to them, in a room they called the library-it was, in fact, his writing-room —whilst the ladies worked. A few evenings after they had recommenced this practice, a discussion arose between Mr. Colman and his eldest daughter, Mary, as to the precise meaning of a French word, and the dictionary had to be appealed to to decide the question. Mary said it was in her bed-chamber, and left the room to fetch it. The library was on the ground-floor, and the staircase was a broad, handsome one as far as the first flight; it had been made by Alfred Zwengler when the house was repaired, and there was a wide landing at the top, the whole being lighted sufficiently for ordinary purposes by a lamp that hung in the hall. The stairs were very easy of ascent, and my mother —I mean Mary-for she was afterwards my mother, who was a lively, active girl, was springing up two steps at a time, when, to her amazement, she saw a gentleman in uniform standing on the landing above. She stopt suddenly, but as he did not appear to notice her, she continued to ascend, concluding it was some stranger, who had got into the house by mistake, for he did not look a thief; but when she reached the landing he was gone. She stood at first bewildered. There were four doors opening into bedrooms, but they were all shut; and after thinking a moment, she concluded it was the shadow of some cloaks and hats, and sticks, that were hanging in the hall, that had deceived her. She did not pause to consider how this could be, but turned into her own room; felt for the book, which she remembered to have left on her bed and ran down stairs again to her father; so occupied with the disputed question, that for the moment she forgot what had happened, and as her father resumed his reading immediately, she did not mention it. When they were going to bed, and they were lighting their candles in the hall, she said, 'you can't think what a start I had this evening when I went for the dictionary. It must have been the shadow of those cloaks and things, but I could have declared I saw an officer in uniform standing at the top of the stairs. I even saw his epaulette and the colour of his clothes.'

"'La! Mary,' said one of the younger ones, 'weren't you frightened?'

"'Frightened! no, why should I be frightened at a shadow?'

"'Or a handsome young officer either,' said one of the boys.

"She playfully gave him a tap on the head, and they all went to bed, thinking no more of the matter.

"The kitchen was at the back of the house, on the same floor as the library, and a few evenings after this occurrence, one of the girls being in the store-room, heard sounds of distress proceeding thence; and on opening the kitchen-door, to inquire what was the matter, she saw Jemima, the English girl, in hysterics, and the other two standing over her, sprinkling her face with water. They said that she had left the kitchen to fetch some worsted to mend her master's stockings, but that before she could have got up stairs, she had rushed back again, thrown herself into a chair, and '*gone off*' as they expressed it. On hearing the noise, Mr. and Mrs. Colman joined them, but, for a long time, they could extract nothing from her-but that she had seen *something*. My grandfather asked if it was a rat, or a robber! but she only shook her head; and it was not till they had all left the kitchen and sent her a glass of wine, that she was sufficiently collected to tell them that, as she got to the foot of the stairs, she saw an officer in uniform, going up before her. He had his cap in his hand, and his sword at his side; and supposing he was some friend of her master's, she was going to follow him up; but when he reached the landing, to her surprise and horror, he disappeared through the wall.

"When the family heard this, combining it with what had happened to Mary-though the circumstance had never been mentioned in the hearing of the servants; nor, indeed, even alluded to a second time-they began to ask themselves whether it was possible any such person could get into the house? and they examined every part of it with care, but found nothing that threw a light on the mystery. After this, Jemima was afraid to go up stairs alone at night, and Gretchen shared her fears; but the Frenchwoman laughed at them both, and said she should like to see a ghost that would frighten her. One night, however, about nine o'clock, when the family were in the library, they suddenly heard a great noise upon the stairs, as if something had fallen from the top to the bottom, and when they all rushed out to see what was the matter, they found the cook lying across the lower step in a state of insensibility, and the coalscuttle upset beside her, with its contents scattered around. They carried her into the library, and when she revived, she insisted on immediately leaving the house; she would not sleep in it another night on any account whatever, and away she went. Gretchen and Jemima said, they were sure she had seen the ghost, but was too proud to own it, after turning their fears into ridicule; and the family began to be very much perplexed.

"My grandfather had a truly philosophical mind, and did not think it a proof of wisdom to hold decided opinions on subjects that he had not investigated. He had never believed in spiritual appearances, but he had never thought seriously on the subject at all, and did not feel himself qualified to assert that such things were impossible. Certainly, it was a singular coincidence, that Jemima's description of the apparition exactly coincided with what my mother had seen; and though the Frenchwoman had confessed to nothing, yet it was at the same hour and the same place that she had taken fright. He tried, whether-by placing the cloaks and the lamp in certain relative positions-he could produce any reflection that might deceive the eye; but there was not the most remote approximation to such a thing; in short, he perceived that that explanation of the appearance was altogether inadmissible.

"'Well,' he said, 'if anybody sees this figure again, I beg they will call me!'

"They were not a nervous family, I suppose; my mother was quite the reverse, I know. I never saw anybody with more courage; at all events, they do not seem to have been alarmed, though both the boys afterwards saw the same figure on the same spot, and ran to call their father; but when Mr. Colman came it was gone. However, they declared they had seen it cross the landing; and that it had seemed to them, to walk through the wall, just as Jemima had described.

"Some weeks after this, towards the same hour, as Mr. Colman was about to commence reading aloud, he discovered that he had left his spectacles in the pocket of his coat, when he dressed for dinner; and my mother, who was always alert and active, left the room to fetch them. Presently, she re-entered the room,—pale, and somewhat agitated, but perfectly collected; and said, that when she had ascended the stairs about half-way, she heard a slight rustle above, which caused her to raise her eyes; when she saw, distinctly, the same figure she had seen before. 'I was not frightened!' she said, 'and I stopt with one foot on the next stair, and looked at it steadily, that I might be sure I was not under a delusion. The face was pale, and it looked at me with such a sad expression, that I thought if it was really a ghost, it might wish to say something; so I asked it.'

"'Asked it!' they all exclaimed. 'What did you say?'

"'I said, if you have anything to communicate, I conjure you-speak!'

"'And did it.'

"'No,' answered Mary, 'but it made a sign—'

"'Good Heavens!' said Mrs. Colman, 'do you know what you're saying?'

"'Perfectly,' said Mary, calmly. 'With one hand it pointed to the wall-just where Jemima and the boys saw it go in-and with the other it made a movement, as if it was going to strike the wall with something heavy.'

"'Perhaps there's some money buried there,' said one of the boys.

"Mr. Colman, who had hitherto been a silent but amazed listener to his daughter's narration, asked her what the gesture appeared to signify.

"'It was as if it wanted the wall to be pulled down-at least, I thought so. I wish I had asked if that was what it wished, but I had not presence of mind; if I see it again, I will.'

"'But we could not pull down the wall, you know, my dear,' said Mrs. Colman.

"'I suppose we might, if we engaged to build it up again,' suggested one of the party.

"'But if we told anybody, we should not get the money,' said the boys.

"'Hush!' said Mary, 'Don't speak in that way; think what a solemn thing it is. I shall never forget his face-never, to the day of my death; and it looked at me so gratefully when I spoke to it, and then it disappeared into the wall.'

"Of course this extraordinary occurrence formed the subject of conversation for the rest of the evening, and Mr. Colman narrowly questioned his daughter with regard to the particulars; but her story was always consistent, and as he had a very high opinion of Mary's courage and sense, the circumstance made so much impression on him, that he set about making enquiries as to the owner and antecedents of the house. It was difficult to obtain much information-for saying a house is haunted, is an injury to the landlord, and sometimes brings people into trouble-but he ascertained that it had had several tenants, that nobody had staid in it long, and that one of the persons who had inhabited it for a short time, was Mr. Bautte himself, whereupon he resolved to pay him a visit.

"Mr. Bautte, as I have mentioned, was a watchmaker; and though very rich, still attended to his trade, so that it was easy to obtain an interview with him. Mr. Colman called at his place of business, which was not a shop, but a room on the first floor of a private house. He asked about the engraving of a seal that he had to his watch-chain; and then, having ascertained which was Mr. B., he told him he was his tenant. Mr. B. bowed and said, 'I hope you like the house, sir.'

"My grandfather said that, perhaps, he might not have observed it but for what had happened, but that he fancied this was said with a sort of misgiving, as if he was conscious that there was something objectionable about the house.

"'Why,' said my grandfather, drawing him rather aside, 'I like the house very much; but there's one great inconvenience about it-we can't get any servants to stay with us. One has left us already, and the others have given us warning, and nobody seems willing to come in their places. I understand you lived in the house yourself a short time; may I ask if you found any similar difficulty?'

"'Well, sir,' said Mr. Bautte, trying to look unconcerned, 'you are aware how ignorant and foolish such people are —I fancy from the construction of the house that the sounds from the next door penetrate the walls.'

"'We hear no sounds,' said Mr. Colman. 'I have heard no complaints of any. Did any of your family ever say they saw anything extraordinary there?'

"'Well, sir, since you put the question so directly, I can't deny that the female part of my family did assert something of the sort; but women have generally a tendency to superstition, and are easily terrified.'

"'Very true,' said Mr. Colman, 'but I should take it as a great favour if you would tell me what they said they saw —I have no idea of leaving the house; you need not be afraid of that; and of course I shall not mention this conversation to any one-what did they say they saw?'

"Mr. Bautte thus exhorted, confessed that his family, and everybody who had lived in the house, asserted that they had seen the apparition of a young man in uniform, who always appeared on the stairs or the landing; adding, that he himself had never seen it, although he had put himself in the way of it repeatedly, and he firmly believed it was some extraordinary delusion or optical deception, though it was impossible to account for its affecting so many persons in the same way.

"My grandfather then told him what had occurred in his family; especially to his eldest daughter, in whose testimony, he assured Mr. Bautte, he placed the greatest reliance; and he ventured to propose an examination of the spot, where the figure was said invariably to disappear.

At first, Mr. Bautte laughed at the idea; for-besides his scepticism, which made him unwilling to take any proceeding that countenanced what he considered an absurd superstition-he urged, that the staircase and landing in question, were of very recent erection, being one of Mr. Zwengler's improvements when he repaired the house. However, after a short argument, wherein my grandfather represented that nobody but the parties concerned need know the real reason for what they did, that the expense would be small, and the possible result beneficial to the property, Mr. Bautte consented, provided Mr. Geierstecke made no objection; he being still the owner of the house.

"Mr. G., who, you know, was my husband's father, was aware that the Hôtel du Pont had frequently changed its tenants, but was quite ignorant of the cause. He had no immediate interest in the matter, as Mr. Bautte held a thirty-years lease, and he naturally assumed that these frequent changes were purely accidental. Everybody, who became acquainted with the house, had a strong motive for keeping the secret; for-besides the ridicule and penalty they might have incurred-they all wanted to get it off their hands. It's true, that amongst the servants and common people of the neighbourhood, there were strange whispers going about; the source of which it would not have been easy to trace. A glazier said he knew a man, who had heard another declare, that he was acquainted with a bricklayer, who had helped to build the staircase; who used to say, he did not wonder that nobody could live in the Hôtel du Pont; and that it was his opinion that nobody ever would be able to live in it; and a woman who kept a shop opposite, had been heard to say, that she saw somebody go into that house that never came out again; but whenever she alluded to this subject, her husband always reproved her, and told her she did not know what she was talking about.

"This gossip had, however, never reached Mr. Geierstecks, and he was exceedingly surprised when Mr. Bautte communicated Mr. Colman's proposal, and the reason of it. He immediately called upon my grandfather, who recited the circumstances to him, and introduced my mother; from whose lips he wished to hear the account of her two rencontres with the ghost; and also, a particular description of its appearance. At the commencement of his visit, he was inclined to be jocular on the subject; but after he had seen my mother, and heard her describe the dress of the apparition, which was that of an officer in the Republican army of France, he seemed a good deal struck, and became serious. He said, he did not believe in ghosts; though he had heard people affirm, that they had seen such things; he always supposed them to be under a delusion; but that my mother's testimony was so clear, and from the account of her family she was so unlikely a person to be deceived, that he felt bound to give his assent to the proposed investigation; only stipulating for entire secrecy, and that he might fix the day for it himself. 'I'll speak to a builder,' said he; 'Mr. Bautte, of course, will wish to be present; and, perhaps, I may bring a friend with me.'

"As I mentioned before, he had been early acquainted with the Zwengler's; and betwixt him and Alfred the intimacy still continued, although the latter was by no means the pleasant companion he had been formerly. Mr. Geierstecke concluding that his uncle's will, and the sudden vicissitudes of fortune he had experienced, had affected his spirits, pitied him; and had often endeavoured to argue him out of his depression, but with little effect.

"I have heard him say, that after he left my grandfather's house on that day, he went to Mr. Zwengler's with the intention of telling him the circumstances I have related, and also of giving him notice of the impending investigation; but when he had got to the door, and his hand was upon the bell, he shrunk from the interview. 'Not,' he said, 'that he admitted a suspicion; on the contrary, he repelled it; but he could not overcome an uneasy feeling at the striking resemblance between Louis Zwengler and the ghost (if ghost there was), as described by my mother. He feared that, if his words did not betray this feeling, his countenance would, and he could not face Alfred in this state of mind; so he turned from the door and went home. Still he felt he could not allow this thing to be done without warning his friend of their intention, and he sat down to write him a letter; but it was a difficult thing to communicate, —at least, he somehow found it so. He could have mentioned it jocularly; but that, under all the circumstances, he could not do so; and he had torn up two or three unsuccessful efforts, when the door opened, and the servant announced Mr. Zwengler himself.

"My father-in-law told me that he felt his knees tremble, and his cheek turn pale, when he rose to receive his visitor, who seemingly rather more cheerful than usual, said he had called to ask him why he did not come in to-day, when he was at his door. 'I was at the window,' said he, 'and was quite disappointed to see you turn away.'

"This was too good an opportunity to be lost, and Mr. Geierstecke answered, that it was quite true, and that he had actually had his hand upon the bell, when he thought it was useless troubling him with such nonsense.

"'What nonsense?' asked Zwengler.

"'It's about that house I bought of you,' said Mr. Geierstecke. 'People say they can't live in it;' adding, while he affected to laugh; 'They say there's a ghost in it, and they want to pull down the staircase to look for him.'

"'How absurd,' said Mr. Zwengler; 'and are you going to do it?' but the voice sounded as if there was something in his throat.

"'We are,' replied Mr. G. 'Mr. Bautte has never been able to keep a tenant, and I can't refuse, for it appears they all assert the same thing. Even Mr. Bautte's family would not live in it-they say they see——'

"'Ha! ha!' laughed Zwengler, rising suddenly, and pushing back his chair in a hurried manner, 'but I must leave you—I've an appointment; I merely called as I passed the door, to ask why you'd not come in. Bless me! I'm late,' he added, as he looked at his watch; and he hurried out of the room, crying 'Good night,' as he disappeared.

"Mr. Geierstecke used to say that he believed that he (Mr. G. himself) continued standing on the same spot, like a statue, for nearly half an hour after the door closed on his visitor.

"'I had scarcely had time to rise from my chair,' he said, 'before he was gone, and I felt paralysed. I did not know what to do. I wished I had never bought the house, and I lay awake all night, thinking of horrors, and then trying to persuade myself that perhaps there was no cause for my apprehensions after all.'

"'I saw nothing more of Zwengler, though I frequently passed his house purposely; and, at length, the day arrived which I had-not without design-fixed at the interval of a week from my first visit to Mr. Colman. We all assembled at the appointed time, with a respectable workman whom I was in the habit of employing, to whom we accounted for our proceeding, by alleging that there was a bad smell sometimes, which we thought might proceed from a dead rat.

"'I never felt more nervous and agitated in my life, than while the man was demolishing the wall, and we were waiting the denouement; while Mary, the heroine, stood pale and earnest, with her eyes eagerly fixed on the spot.'

"'We had better have a light, sir,' said the mason presently, 'There is something here——'

"One of the boys went for a light, while silent and breathless they waited its arrival.

"When it came it disclosed a fearful sight. There lay, huddled up, as if thrust in in haste, the bones of a perfect skeleton, and what appeared to be burnt remnants of clothes. Before they touched anything, Mr. Bautte sent for the police, and these sad relics were removed by their officers. There was no means of discovering how life had been taken, but the medical men said that some strong chemical preparation had been used to consume the flesh and clothes, and prevent any bad odour.

"Everybody knew the Zwenglers and their history; and on this discovery, the prefêt sent for my mother, and took her deposition as to the appearance of the figure she had seen. He also examined Jemima and the Frenchwoman who had left our service; and the testimony of all parties coinciding, he issued an order to arrest Alfred. But when they went to his house he was not there. The servants said he had been absent nearly a week; that he left, saying he was going on business to Dôle, and his stay was uncertain. He had taken no baggage with him but a carpet bag. A messenger was despatched to Dôle, but nothing was known of him there; and the enquiries that were instituted at the Messageries and Voituriers threw no light on his mode of conveyance, if, indeed, he had left Geneva.

"Various people, who had lived in the house, now confessed to have been troubled with the same apparition; and several amongst the neighbours of the lower ranks avowed that they had strong suspicions that Alfred Zwengler did not come fairly by his fortune, alleging different reasons for their opinion; one of which was singular-it was, that a little deaf and dumb girl, who lived near him, described to her mother, that when he passed their door, she always saw him as enveloped in a black cloud.

"Howbeit, Alfred Zwengler never appeared more; and it was generally thought that terrified by the impending disclosure he had thrown himself either into the lake or the river, to escape it. He left no will, and the fortune went to his sisters. But this strange circumstance resulted in my mother's marriage to Monsieur de Beaugarde the Prefect, who was so captivated by her courage, that he made her an offer immediately; and the acquaintance with Mr. Geierstecke, thus commenced, led to my marriage with his son."

In answer to my enquiry, of how it was supposed the murder was committed, Madame de G. said, the conjecture was, that Louis had made his escape from the Chouans, and returned unexpectedly—a neighbour even testified to having seen him enter the house one night at the time it was under repair-and that his brother by a sudden and dreadful impulse, had struck him down unawares. One of the masons who had been employed in building the staircase, but who was killed by a fall shortly before the discovery, had been heard to hint that before he died he must unburden his mind of a secret that weighed heavily on his conscience. "Not that the guilt lies on my soul, he used to say, but perhaps it's a sin to hold my tongue."

However, he had no time to speak; but one came from the grave to tell the tale and bear awful witness against the unhappy Alfred Zwengler.

The Sheep-Farmer's Story

The following singular story was related to me in a dialect which, though I understood, from having lived much in the country where it was spoken, I cannot attempt to imitate, not being "to the manner born;" neither, if I could, would it be agreeable, or very comprehensible, to my readers in general. I shall, therefore, tell it in plain English; and hope it will interest others as much as it did me.

Sandy Shiels, the narrator, was a sheep-farmer in the Lammermuirs. He lived in a lone house, in a wild and desolate country, with his wife and children, his farm-servants, and his dogs, and seldom saw a stranger enter his door, from week's end to week's end; but on certain occasions, more or less frequent, Sandy attended the fairs and markets about the country; and at the cattle shows, sometimes, appeared in Edinburgh itself. He was a shrewd and a simple man-for the two characteristics are by no means incompatible-hardhanded and hardfeatured, but not unkindly; a serious churchman, a great reader of his Bible, and a keen observer of Nature and Nature's language, as men who are born and bred amongst mountains generally are.

His wife was a plain, hardworking woman, by whom he had two children, yet young; but he had an elder son by a former marriage, called Ihan Dhu; a Highland appellation not common in the Lammermuirs; but his mother was a Highland woman, and had given it to him. Ihan Dhu means Black John; and it suited him well; for, instead of the brawny figure and sandy hue which so generally prevails in the south, he had inherited the slight figure, the dark complexion, and black hair and eyes of his mother, who was a specimen of the genuine Highland type; which, contrary to the belief commonly entertained in England, is (Lord Jeffrey informed me), *a little dark man.*

The two farm-servants were called Donald and Rob. The former a heavy, stolid lout, who had just intellect enough to do what he was told; the latter, a smart, lively, goodnatured lad, who was fond of reading, when he could get a book; and wide awake about everything that his very limited sphere brought him in contact with. The only other member of the family was a girl, called Annie Goil, an orphan niece of Mrs. Shiel's; who, in conjunction with her aunt, did all the work of the house and dairy. The whole household lived and ate, and sat together, and with them the two sheep dogs, Coully and Jock. In the summer, it was pleasant enough; but in the winter, when the snow fell and the sheep were on the hills, they had often a hard time of it.

Annie Goil was a pretty lass; and, naturally enough, there being no other at hand, the three young men, Ihan, Donald, and Rob, were all candidates for her favour. Nevertheless, they lived tolerably well together; the rivalry, apparently, not running very high. Ihan was, of course, much the best match; and he might, perhaps, feel pretty confident that whenever he chose seriously to put in his claim, it could not be resisted. Rob, possibly, comforted and consoled himself with the sundry little marks of preference she bestowed on him, which might be genuine, or might be designed to *agacer* Ihan. As for Donald, he was of so slow and undemonstrative a nature, that though she and the other two often jeered him, and pretended to think he was the one destined to carry off the prize, he exhibited neither anger nor jealousy; if he felt either, he kept them to himself.

Nevertheless, a sharp word, or sour look, would occasionally pass between them; that is, between Ihan and Rob; for any dissatisfaction on the part of Donald was only expressed by increased stolidity and silence; and so persuaded was the old man that their feelings towards each other were not very genial; to say the least, that he had been heard to say to his wife, that Annie Goil was a good girl; but, perhaps, it would have been better, if she had never come amongst them.

Still they rubbed on "middling well," as Sandy said, and certainly far better than might have been expected under such circumstances.

The winter preceding the circumstances I am about to relate, had been a very severe one, and Sandy Shiels, who had exposed himself too much to the weather, was laid up with an attack of rheumatism. As he was a very active man, still not much past middle life, who when in health diligently looked after his business himself; his loss during this confinement was much felt; and the others had enough to do to make up for his absence.

On the 27th of February, the snow was on the ground, and the wind blew wildly over the Lammermuir hills; the sheep sought shelter and munched their turnips sadly in the nooks and hollows. Donald was abroad, with the dogs looking after them, and seeing that no stray lamb perished in the cold; while Ihan and Rob were off to Gifford. Ihan to do business there for his father; for there was a three days fair, or market, which Sandy, when in health, never failed to attend, both as a buyer and seller; and Rob to fetch some medicine for the patient, and other matters wanted at the farm.

Rob set out at dawn of day, for it was a long walk of ten miles through the snow, and the sooner he could return the better, as the things he was to bring were wanted. Ihan rode a rough little Shetland pony; he did not start till midday, and was not expected back till the evening after the next. On the first day he had to go on as far as Haddington, which is four miles beyond Gifford, where he was to consult a lawyer about a disputed point in his father's lease. He was to sleep there at the house of a friend, and to be back to the Gifford market early the next morning.

Annie Goil stood at the door covertly watching Ihan as he mounted his pony, well equipt for his cold ride, his neck enveloped in a red comforter, knitted for him by Annie herself. She leant against the door-post looking about her with an air of indifference; while Ihan seemed wholly occupied in tightening his girths and seeing that his stirrups were of the right length. Neither spoke; still he lingered over his gear, and still she stood leaning against the post, when suddenly Mrs. Shiels called from above, "Is Ihan gone? Stop him!" and hurrying down stairs appeared at the door.

"Ihan," she said, "I forgot to tell Rob to bring sixpennyworth of camphorated spirits for your father; if he has not left Gifford before you get there, tell him to get it."

"He will have left, I should think," answered Ihan.

"Perhaps not," said Mrs. Shiels, "but if he has you must bring it, though I want it to night."

"Very well," said Ihan as he rode away, and Mrs. Shiels and Annie re-entered the house.

The hours passed drearily at the farm, with the sick man groaning in his pain, and the two lonely women dividing their time betwixt his chamber and their household cares. As the day advanced Annie went frequently to the door and looked up the glen; and Mrs. Shiels, glancing at the Dutch timepiece that stood in the kitchen, observed that she wondered Rob had not come back. Annie responding that the snow was deep, and it must be very heavy walking, again went to the door and looked up the glen; but there was nobody in sight. The hours dragged on, and as it grew later, large flakes began to fall and obscure what little light remained. Sandy grew impatient and accused Rob of idling and lingering at the fair; Mrs. Shiels wondered; and Annie having done her work, took up her station at the door with her gown-skirt over her head; there she stood listening for the sound of a step, for it was too dark to see, and at last, she heard a heavy foot approaching, but it was Donald returning from the hills, followed by Jock.

"You haven't seen anything of Rob, have you?" said Annie.

"How should I see Rob! He's gone to Gifford ar'n't he?"

"You might have been on that side of the hill?"

"Ar'n't he come back with the stuff?"

"No; he might have been here three hours since. I can't think what's become of him."

"Stopt at the Fair, may-be; there's dancing the night at the Lion."

"Nonsense!" said Annie, pouting her lips at him, and turning away to prepare their evening meal.

Donald shook himself, and stamped his feet to get rid of the snow, and then entered the kitchen. Mrs. Shiels hearing a foot, came down, hoping to find Rob; and was very much disappointed when she saw it was Donald.

"What can that boy be doing, all this time?" she said.

"Perhaps he met Ihan, and went back for the camphor," suggested Annie.

"He'd never think of such a thing! Ihan would not let him; that is, if he had got any way on," said Mrs. Shiels.

"There's dancing the night at the Lion," reiterated Donald.

"Why, the boy would never think of staying for that!" exclaimed Mrs. Shiels; indignant at the mere notion of such a disorderly proceeding.

"To be sure, he wouldn't," said Annie; "Donald knows that well enough;" and her lip curled as she spoke!

Annie was evidently disturbed at Rob's prolonged absence, and angry with Donald's insidious attempts to put an ill construction on it. But still Rob did not come.

Annie went on preparing the supper, which consisted of porridge; and when she had poured it into the bowls, she made two messes for the dogs.

"Where's Coullie?" she said looking round.

"Arn't he here?" inquired Donald.

"No.—Don't you see he's not?"

"Well, I thought he came in with me," said Donald; and going to the door he began whistling the familiar whistle that calls home the dogs. Jock leaving his bowl of porridge, that Annie had set down, went to the door too. Presently they both returned; Donald sat down to his supper, saying, he supposed the dog would come presently; and Jock applied himself to his.

As the night drew on, the wonders and conjectures increased, and the family grew more and more fidgity and perplexed at Rob's absence. Donald went to bed as he had to be up betimes in the morning; Mrs. Shiels did the same, because she slept in her sick husband's room; Annie lingered as long as she could; then she made up a good fire, set a saucepan of porridge on the hob, left a bowl and a spoon, and salt on the table, and went to bed too. When she was undrest and had extinguished her candle, she opened the lattice window of her chamber and put out her head. The snow still fell, and it was very dark; after listening for some minutes, she shut the window, and softly opening her chamber door, she crept down stairs again to the kitchen. There she unhooked a lantern from the wall, put a lighted candle in it, and returning to her room, she hung it on the latch of the window before she got into bed. She thought she should not sleep, but after a little while she did, and soundly too, till next morning. When she opened her eyes at dawn of day, the candle was burnt out, but the sight of the lantern in so unusual a place, reminded her immediately why she had placed it there, and she wondered whether Rob had come home in the night, and been let in by Donald. When she came down, Donald was already outside the house cleaning his shoes and feeding the pigs. She called to him, "Is Rob come?"

"I don't know," he answered. Of course, then, he was not. It was most extraordinary.

"Is Coullie come in?" she asked.

"I ha'nt seen him," he said.

He was very silent; swallowed his mess of porridge in haste, and then set off to the hills with Jock. When Mrs. Shiels came down, the same questions were reiterated; and when she found Rob was not come, she was very angry, and expressed her conviction that he had staid for the dance at the Lion. Even Annie no longer defended him, for where else could he be all night? A pretty rating he will get when he comes back thought she; and she could not deny that he well deserved it.

She expected him early, and every now and then she went to the door as on the preceding day; but hour after hour passed, and he did not come. All sorts of conjectures were formed as to the cause of the delay, but Mrs. Shiels and her husband admitted but one solution of the difficulty—"the boy's head had got clean turned, and he was gone to the bad althegither."

At night, Donald came home to the great surprise of all, without Coullie; he said he had seen nothing of the dog. Now Coullie was devoted to Rob-in short, he was the only person the animal cared for-and it occurred to Annie that he had somehow come upon Rob's footsteps, and tracked him to Gifford, and she expected whenever they did come, to see them both arrive together.

But that night passed and the next day, and then, towards evening, Annie, who had been to the door, announced that she heard the pony's foot; here was at hand one who doubtless would be able to solve the mystery about the absentee. It was the first question addressed to him —"Where's Rob?"

"How should I know?"

"Haven't you seen him?"

"Seen him, no; I've not seen him since the day before yesterday. Why? what's the matter?"

"He's never come back from Gifford. Where was he when you saw him?"

"I never saw him at all, except in the morning before he set off."

"You did not meet him on the road, nor in the village?"

"No; I saw nothing of him after he left this."

"Did you hear if he had been there?"

"I never asked; I bought the camphor-here it is. How's father?"

At night, Donald came home, still without Coullie; and as the dog had never strayed before, it was natural to conclude that he had gone after Rob, wherever the latter might be. The irritation of Mr. and Mrs. Shiels increased hourly, so did Annie's wonder and perplexity. The two young men, Ihan and Donald, were differently affected; Ihan seemed rather pleased, and he covertly taunted Annie with this desertion of her favourite; Donald was only more silent and stolid than he had been before.

But the next day, and the next passed, and so on through the winter, and neither the man nor the dog were seen or heard of. It was ascertained by enquiry that he had been at Gifford, and made his purchases, and it was supposed, had left it early, but *that* no one knew. Certainly, he was not at the ball at the Lion. Somebody had seen him in company with a young man from Edinburgh, in a tax cart, but nobody knew who he was; and, finally, Mr. and Mrs. Shiels declared their conviction that, tempted by fine promises-being an ambitious lad-he had gone off to Edinburgh with this acquaintance, to better his fortune; and Ihan appeared to adopt their opinion. Annie had considerable difficulty in doing so; but, at length, even she ceased to defend him, since there was no other way of accounting for his absence.

Before the winter was over, Donald had left. He had come home one night, with his hands dreadfully mangled by a pole-cat, which he said he had found devouring a rabbit under a bush, and had rashly attempted to lay hold of. Hereupon, he went away to the infirmary in Edinburgh, to be under Dr. S.; and Sandy Shiels engaged a man to fill his situation, and also bought a dog in place of Coullie, whose loss he much regretted, well-broken sheep dogs being very valuable.

Some time had elapsed-the fine weather had set in; and with it, the farmer had got rid of his rheumatism, and resumed his former habits of active occupation; when one day, as he was crossing the hill between his own farm and a place called 'The Hopes,' he observed a dog trotting along, that struck him as being very like Coullie. He gave a whistle, and the animal stopt and looked round, and on calling him by his name, he came up and fondled his master, appearing very glad to see him, and finally accompanying him where he was going.

'The Hopes' was a gentleman's house, about three miles from Shiels' farm, and when he reached the gate, he was surprised to hear the keeper at the lodge say, patting the dog familiarly, "Well, Willie, so you've come back again?" Whereupon Sandy asked him if he knew him.

"Oh, yes, I know him," he said; "he's a great favourite of the ladies here. They found him on the hill nearly starved, some time ago, and he followed them home, and has lived here, off and on, ever since."

"That's very odd," said Sandy, "for the dog's mine. I brought him up from a pup, and we broke him ourselves-that is, a lad did, that lived with me then, called Rob. But, one day last winter, the lad disappeared, and the dog too, and I've never seen either of them since, till just now I saw the dog on the hill."

"Well," said the keeper, "I think it was early in March the ladies brought him home here. He often goes away; but he comes back again, and the ladies take him along with them when they walk out."

Sandy could not conceive why the dog had deserted his home, or why he had remained starving on the hill, when he knew very well where his food awaited him. The keeper agreed in its being very extraordinary, since he must have known his way over every part of the moor for miles round; and suggested that he might have gone after the young man who had disappeared, and been on his way back, when the ladies met him; but, even if that were so, why had he not returned home since, especially as he was frequently absent for hours, and sometimes all night?

When Sandy Shiels had concluded his business, and was about to depart, he whistled the dog, who followed him willingly enough; but as he approached his own house, Coullie shrunk behind, and seemed inclined to turn tail, and run away; however, he came on in obedience to his master's call, and was joyfully received by the family in general, who listened with interest to the account of his adventures, as far as they were known; all agreeing that his absence must, in some way, be connected with that of Rob. It was observed that one of his first movements was to examine the premises after his own fashion, sniffing about, first below, and afterwards above stairs in the attic in which Rob and Donald formerly slept. What was the result of these investigations we cannot tell; but when they were concluded, he stretched himself before the kitchen fire, and went to sleep.

The following days, Sandy took him on the hill when he went to look at the sheep, and he did his duty as formerly; but on the third or fourth evening he was missed, and was absent all night. He returned in the morning, and was gently chided for this irregularity-the family concluding he had been to visit his friends at "The Hopes;" however, a few evenings after, when they were sitting at supper, with the doors closed, and the dogs lying quietly dozing on the hearth, Coullie suddenly started up, and began to show signs of uneasiness; while, almost at the same moment, something like a low whistle reached their ears, which seemed to proceed from the air, rather than the earth. They had heard no sound of footsteps, but Ihan rose from the table and opened the door; whereupon Coullie seized the opportunity to dart out, and Ihan returned, saying he could see nobody, but that Coullie was off at the rate of ten miles an hour. Everybody wondered where he was gone; and at last it was concluded that some person from 'The Hopes' had been passing near the house, and that the dog had recognised the whistle, and followed him. The truant was found at the door in the morning, and chided as before, but that did not prevent his repeating the offence, till their wonder was greatly increased by the following circumstance: —

Sandy Shiels always read prayers to his family on the Sunday evenings; and one night, while he was thus engaged, and the dogs were lying apparently asleep, Coullie suddenly uttered two or three low whines. Annie raised her head from her book to bid him be silent, and observing that he was sitting up, looking eagerly towards the door, which was open, she turned her eyes in that direction, and saw to her astonishment, a man standing in the dusk of the passage. As all the inmates of the house were present, and the outer door was shut, so that no stranger could have come in, she uttered an exclamation of surprise which interrupted the reader, and caused everybody to turn their heads; but with the sound of her voice the figure had disappeared, and the others saw nothing. Coullie ran to the door, and became uneasy, while Sandy asked what was the matter.

"I saw a man in the passage," said Annie, looking very pale and agitated.

"A man," said Ihan, rising; "I saw no man;" and going into the passage, he opened the outer door to look round; whereupon, Coullie seized the opportunity, and rushed out.

"There's nobody that I see," said Ihan; "but the dog's off again."

"I'm sure I saw somebody," said Annie.

"Go and look up stairs," said Mrs. Shiels; Ihan went and returned, saying there was nobody in the house but themselves, and Annie must have been mistaken.

But Annie shook her head, and beginning to cry, asserted that she had not been mistaken, and that she believed the man she saw was Rob, adding, that she always thought that the whistle they sometimes heard, and which agitated Coullie so much, was Rob's whistle.

At this suggestion, Ihan fired and showed symptoms of great irritation; and if Sandy had not been present, high words would have arisen betwixt him and Annie. As it was, his countenance was clouded all the rest of the evening.

This event made a great impression on the young girl; she thought of it day and night, and she watched with increasing interest Coullie's inexplicable proceedings, which still continued. Sometimes of an evening they would hear footsteps, whereon the dog would betray great uneasiness till they opened the door, and he could dart off on his mysterious errand. Once or twice they confined him and would not let him go; but the animal seemed so much distressed and whined so piteously, that they ceased to oppose his inclinations. Although when they heard these footsteps they searched the premises in all directions, nobody was ever to be found. Annie wished them to endeavour to find out where Coullie went; but nobody seemed to have sufficient curiosity to take any trouble about the matter, though they all admitted the singularity of the circumstances. No doubt, it was difficult, inasmuch as he always started on these expeditions at night, while he ran off so rapidly that it would have been impossible to overtake him or keep him in sight. This state of things continued till the month of October, which became very cold; and one morning, towards the end of it, Annie, when she went to the door, found there had been a fall of snow in the night. Coullie, who had gone off the evening before, was there waiting to be let in, and she observed the track of his feet on the ground. It immediately occurred to her that here was an opportunity of discovering what she wished so much to know. She had nobody to consult, for her aunt and uncle were not come down; and being a stout country girl, she threw her shawl over her head, and calling the dog to follow her, she set off up hill and down dale, guided by the marks of Coullie's footsteps which remained perfectly distinct for about four miles in the direction of Gifford, when they turned off to the left, and stopt at the edge of an old quarry. The dog, who had trotted cheerily beside her, now began to descend into the hollow, stopping and looking up every now and then, whining as if inviting her to follow; but after several attempts she found the descent too steep. When at the bottom, Coullie disappeared for a minute or two under the embankment, and she heard him still whining; but finding she could make no further investigations without assistance, she called the dog who joined her directly, and they returned home to find Mrs. Shiels in a dreadful state of mind at Annie's unaccountable and unprecedented absence. However, when she communicated the cause of it, and the discovery she had made, Sandy was sufficiently aroused to say that he would send some one down to examine the quarry. He did so, and the result was that they found the remains of poor Rob under circumstances that led to the conclusion that he had somehow gone out of his way, and fallen into the pit; for on medical examination, it appeared that both his legs were broken. As the quarry was abandoned and in a lonely spot, a person might very possibly die there under such circumstances without being able to make his distress known.

Poor Rob's remains were committed to the earth; Coullie left off his erratic habits and became an ordinary, but intelligent, sheep dog; and the family at Shiel's farm, after due comment, on the singular events that had led to the discovery of his body, which could only be accounted for by admitting a spiritual agency (a view of the case which Ihan always repelled with scorn) turned their thoughts into other channels, with the exception of Annie, who had a strong persuasion that Rob had not come fairly by his end; and oftentimes she would say to Coullie when alone with the dog, "Ah, Coullie, if you had a tongue that could speak, I think you could tell a tale!"

And Coullie looked at her with his large wise eyes full of affection; for she petted and cherished him for Rob's sake, and always gave him the largest mess at supper time.

Sometimes, too, Annie had strange thoughts about Ihan; he had become more dark, and silent, and sulky, since Rob's death; was it because he was jealous of the interest she had exhibited, or was it from any other cause? Did he meet Rob that day on his way to Gifford? What could Rob be doing so much out of the road as the Quarry? These thoughts naturally made her more and more cold to Ihan, whilst her reserve aggrivated his ill-temper and dissatisfaction.

And Annie was not the only person to whom these questions suggested themselves. People would gossip amongst themselves secretly; it got abroad that there had been a good deal of jealousy amongst the young men, and it was whispered that the first Mrs. Shiels had aptly named her son when she called him Ihan Dhu-Black John. At length, these reports reached Sandy Shiels and his son; the latter appeared sullenly indifferent, but they made the old man very unhappy; and every night when he prayed aloud with the family before retiring to rest, he besought God, saying, "Oh Lord if it be thy pleasure, may them that are innocent be justified!"

At term time, when, in Scotland, servants frequently, especially farm servants, change their situations, the man whom Shiels had engaged in Donald's place left; and having heard that Donald, who had been in service at Dunse, was leaving also, Sandy wrote and proposed to him to return; the proposal was accepted, and they were expecting him, when a cart was heard to stop at the door, out of which they looked to see him alight; but the visitor proved to be an old Highland woman who introduced herself as Rob's grandmother-his father and mother having emigrated. She said she had heard the account of her boy's death, and the attachment displayed by the dog, and that she had come all the way to see the animal, and had brought the money to purchase him; if his master did not object. She had travelled from Argyleshire to Haddington by coach; and at the latter place she had hired a cart and a lad to drive her to her destination. She added that she and her old man "were no that puir but that they could afford to buy the dog that had been so faithful to their ain boy."

Sandy Shiels and his family made her welcome; invited her to stay and take a day or two's repose after her journey, and granted her request with regard to Coullie. Annie was very much interested in the old woman; and the latter was deeply impressed with the circumstances the young girl related to her; enquiring minutely into every particular of places and persons connected with the boy's death. She said it was "wonderfu';" adding, that she had "seen" Rob's funeral,—meaning by the second sight—"but not the manner of his death; but she had no doubt God would shew it her before she died."

On the third day she departed; and Sandy Shiels, who had business at Gifford, drove her and Annie, who wished to accompany her, in his cart. They started in time to meet the coach, Coullie making the fourth passenger; and in due time reached the village and drove up to the door of the Lion, where three or four men were sitting on the bench outside smoking and drinking beer; but the moment the cart stopped-almost before it had stopped-Coullie bounded out of it and with indescribable fury attacked one of the men. His master called him, but he was deaf to his voice; and so violent was his rage that it was not without the assistance of the others that he could draw him off. Even then, whilst holding him back with an iron grasp, the dog growled and shewed his teeth, and with flashing eyes, struggled to renew the onslaught.

"Wha's that?" asked the old woman, who had witnessed the scene with surprise.

"That's our Donald, that I told you of-he that lived with us in poor Rob's time," said Annie. "What a very extraordinary thing of Coullie to do! I never saw him in such a way before. Besides, he couldn't have forgotten Donald!"

"Forget him!" exclaimed the old woman; "Na, na; Coullie no forgets. Mind ye lass; tak tent o' that man-there's bluid upon him!"

Donald in the mean time had retreated into the house in search of some water to wash his hand that Coullie had bitten. When he came out the old woman and the dog had departed.

But the lookers on were not uninterested observers of what had past. A new idea struck them; the tide of opinion was rather turned in Ihan's favour. However, this was but the under current of gossip. Donald went home with Sandy Shiels and Annie, who whatever they might have thought, said nothing; but after this, in the nightly prayer, Sandy not only besought God that the innocent might be justified; but also, that the guilty might be brought to repentance; and sometimes he would go further, dilating on the duties enjoined by a *true* repentance; such as reparation, where reparation could be made; and, at all events, where it could not, taking the burthen of our guilt on our own shoulders, even though it weigh us down to death, rather than let the guiltless man suffer, though it were only the breath of slander.

One morning, about three weeks after the departure of the old Highland woman, when they opened the door they found Coullie waiting to be let in. However, kindly treated by his new owners, he had found his way back; a letter arrived from them shortly afterwards, saying, they had missed him, and that they did not doubt that he would reach his former home, "and, may, be yet give testimony agen the wicked."

Annie kept the contents of this epistle to herself, but it did not escape her eye that Donald seemed cowed by Coullie's enmity, which the animal never failed to exhibit as much as he durst. Moreover, as time passed, Donald lost his appetite and the healthy hue of his complexion; in short it was evident he was far from happy in his situation; and she thought that Sandy's significant and awful prayers were eating into his soul and wearing him away.

Farm servants are usually hired for six months; and at last Donald gave warning that he should leave next term-he did not think the place agreed with him; so it seemed indeed; but that was the year 1832; and ere term time arrived, the cholera came, and seized upon Donald as one of its first victims in those parts.

Before he died, he made his confession in presence of the doctor, to the effect, that he was jealous of Rob, because in the morning he and Ihan had overheard a conversation between him and Annie, and she had promised him a lock of her hair. That he met him as he was returning from Gilford, induced him to go out of his road towards the Quarry, by saying one of the sheep had fallen in, and when Rob was off his guard, he pushed him over; but not without a desperate struggle, Rob being very active and strong.

He was dreadfully frightened, and ran from the place not knowing what would happen, and for some time he hourly expected Rob to come home. But at length finding he did not, he ventured to approach the spot; but Coullie was there and he flew at him and bit him so severely that he resolved to leave the country and go to the Infirmary. He had heard of Rob's remains being found and buried, while he was living at Dunse; and thinking there would be no more enquiry about the matter, he accepted the farmer's offer to come back, because he wanted to see Annie.

And so he died, justifying the innocent, according to the old man's prayers; but Ihan did not long survive. Sandy said he feared he had taken to whiskey drinking from disappointment and vexation, and the cholera found him also an easy prey.

My Friend's Story

"I don't know how often you have promised to tell me a remarkable thing in the ghostly line, that happened to yourself," said I, the other day to my friend; "but something has always come in the way; now I shall be very much obliged to you for the particulars, if you have no objection to my printing the story."

"None," she said, "but as regards names of persons and places; the circumstances are so singular that I think they deserve to be recorded. That part of the affair which happened to myself I vouch for; and I can only say that I have most entire confidence in the truth of the rest, and that all the enquiries I made, tended to confirm the story.

"I remember your asking me once, why I so seldom visited our place in S — —, and I told you it was because it was so dreadfully *triste* that I could not inhabit it. You will perhaps suppose that what I am going to relate happened there, but it did not, for the house has not even the recommendation of being haunted-that would at least give it an interest-but I am sorry to say the sole interest it possesses is, that it happens to be ours. Dull as it is, however, we lived there shortly after I was married, for some time. I had no children then, which made it all the duller, particularly when my husband was called away; and on one of these occasions, some acquaintances I had, who were living at a place called the Bellfry, about two miles distant, invited me to visit them for a few days.

"The Bellfry is a common place square house, just such as the doctor or lawyer would inhabit in a provincial town; a little white swing gate, a round grass plot, with a few straggling dahlias, a gravel road leading to the small portico, and a terrible loud bell to ring, when you want to be admitted. So much for the exterior. The interior is not at all more suggestive to the fancy. On the ground floor, there is the usual parlour on one side, and drawing-room on the other, with a long passage leading to the offices at the back; upstairs, a sort of corridor, with dingy bedrooms opening into it. Decidedly not lively, but perfectly prosaic, it was by no means calculated to inspire ghostly terrors; and, indeed, I must confess the supernatural, as it is called, was a subject that, at that time, had never engaged my attention. I mention all this to show you that what happened was not 'the offspring of my excited imagination,' as the learned always tell you these things are. Moreover, I was young; and, to the best of my belief, in very good health.

"The room they gave me was the best. It was plainly but comfortably furnished, with a large four-post bed, and it looked into the churchyard; but this is not an uncommon prospect in country towns, and I thought nothing about it. Now that we understand these things better, I should think it not ghostly, but unhealthy.

"The first two or three nights I slept there, nothing particular occurred; but on the fourth or fifth night, soon after I had fallen asleep, I was awoke by a noise which appeared very near me, and on listening attentively, I heard a rustling sound, and footsteps on the floor. I forgot for the moment that I had locked my door, and concluding it was the housekeeper, who sometimes looked in when I was going to bed, to ask if I was comfortable, I said, 'Is that you, Mrs. H?' But there was no answer, upon which I sat up and looked around; and seeing nobody, though I heard the sound still, I jumped out of bed. Then I observed, for if was a bright moonlight night, that there was a large tree in the churchyard, which grew very close to the window, and I concluded that a breeze had arisen, and caused the branches to touch the glass; so I got into bed again quite satisfied, and settled myself to sleep. But scarcely had I closed my eyes, when the footsteps began again, much too distinct this time to be mistaken for anything else; and whilst I was listening in amazement, I heard a heavy, heavy sigh. I had raised myself on my elbow, in order to have my ears freer to listen, and presently I saw the curtains at the foot of the bed, which were closed, slowly and gently opened. I saw no figure, but they were held apart, apparently by the two hands of some one standing there. I bounded out of bed, and rushed out of the room into the corridor, screaming for help. All who heard me, got up and came out of their rooms, to enquire what had happened; but I had not courage to tell the truth, I was afraid of giving offence, or incurring ridicule, and I said I had been awakened by a noise in my room, and I was afraid somebody was concealed there. They went in with me and searched; of course, nobody was found; and one suggested that it was a mouse, another that it was a dream, and so forth. But then, and still more the next morning, I fancied, from their manner, they were better acquainted with my midnight visitor than they chose to say. However, I changed my room, and soon after quitted the Bellfry, which I have never slept at since, so there concludes the story, so far as I am concerned; but there is a sequel to the tale.

"I must tell you that I never mentioned these circumstances, because I knew I should only be laughed at; besides I thought it might annoy my hosts, as they had an idea of going abroad for some time, and it might have interfered with their letting the house.

"Now to my sequel.

"Two or three years after this occurrence, I fell desperately ill; first I was confined of an infant which did not survive; and then I was attacked with typhus fever, which raged in the neighbourhood. I was at death's door for eleven weeks, and not expected to recover; but you see, I did, *nonobstant messrs. les medicins*; but I was so long regaining my strength, that I was recommended to try the effects of a sea voyage. Even then, I could not sit up, and was lifted about like a baby; and as a fine lady's maid would have been of no use on board the yacht, a sailor's daughter from the coast was engaged to attend me; a strong, healthy young woman, to whom my weight was a feather. She tended me most faithfully, and I found her simple, truthful, and straightforward; insomuch, that I had thoughts of engaging her in my service permanently. With this view, and also because it helped to pass the time, I questioned her about her family, and the manner of life of her class, in the out of the way part of the country from which she came.

"'I suppose, Mary, you've never been away from home before?'

"'Oh, yes, Ma'am; I was in service as housemaid for a short time at the Bellfry, not far from your place, Ma'am; but I soon left that, and I have never been out again.'

"'But why did you leave? Didn't you like the place?'

"'No, Ma'am.'

"'But why? Perhaps you'd too much to do?'

"'No, Ma'am, it wasn't a hard place; but unpleasant things happened, and so I left.'

"'What sort of unpleasant things?' said I, my own adventure there suddenly recurring to my memory.

"She hesitated, and said, that perhaps it would alarm me; she had also made a sort of promise to her master and mistress not to talk about it, and she never had mentioned what happened except to her parents, in order to account for leaving so suddenly. I assured her that I should not be alarmed, and overcame her scruples, and then she told me what follows.

"It appeared that she was engaged as housemaid at the Bellfry about two years before my visit there. Shortly after her arrival, her mistress being taken very unwell, her master went to sleep at the other side of the house, whilst Mary made her bed in the dressing-room, in order to be near at hand if the invalid required any assistance in the night. She had directions to keep some refreshment ready in case it was wanted, and towards two o'clock in the morning, her mistress saying she should like a little broth, Mary rose, and half drest, proceeded down stairs with a candle in her hand, to fetch some which she had left simmering on the kitchen fire. As she descended the last flight of stairs, she was a good deal startled at seeing a bright light issuing from the kitchen-the door of which was open-much brighter than could possibly proceed from the fire, for the whole passage was illuminated by it. Her first and very natural idea was that there were thieves in the house; and she was about to rush upstairs again to her master's room, when it occurred to her that one of the servants might be sitting up for some object of her own, and she stopt to listen, but there was not the least sound-all was silent. It then occurred to her that possibly something might have caught fire; so half-frightened, she advanced on tip-toe and peeped in, when, to her surprise, she saw a lady dressed in white, sitting by the fire, into which she was sadly and thoughtfully gazing. Her hands were clasped upon her knees, and two large greyhounds-beautiful dogs, said Mary-sat at her feet, both looking up fondly in her face.

Her dress seemed to be of cambric or dimity, and from Mary's description, was that worn by ladies in the seventeenth century.

"The kitchen was as bright as if illuminated by twenty candles, but this did not strike her she said, till afterwards; so quite reassured by the appearance of a lady instead of a band of robbers, it did not occur to her to question who she was or how she came there; and saying, 'I beg your pardon ma'am', she entered the kitchen, dropt a curtsey, and was going towards the fire, but as she advanced the vision retreated, till, at last, lady, chair, and dogs, glided through the closed window; and then the figure appeared standing erect in the garden, with its face close to the panes, and the eyes looking sorrowfully and earnestly on poor Mary.

"'And what did you do then, Mary?' said I.

"'Oh, ma'am, then I *fared* to feel very queer, and I fell upon the floor with a scream.'

"Her master heard the cry, and came down to see what was the matter. When she told him what she had seen, he endeavoured to persuade her it was all fancy; but Mary said she knew better than that; however, she promised not to talk of it, as it might frighten her sick mistress.

"Subsequently, she met the same melancholy apparition pacing the corridor into which the room that I had slept in opened; and not liking these rencontres she gave warning and left the place.

"She knew nothing more, for her home was at some distance from the Bellfry, which she had not since revisited: but when I had recovered my health and returned to that part of the country, I found, on enquiry, that this apparition was believed to haunt not only the house, but the neighbourhood; and I conversed with several people who affirmed they had seen her, generally alone, but sometimes accompanied by the two dogs.

"One woman said she had no fear, and that she had determined if she met the ghost, to try and touch her, in order to ascertain if it was positively an apparition; she did meet her in the dusk of the evening on the path that runs by the high road between the Bellfry and G—— and put out her arm to take hold of her dress. She felt no substance, but she described the sensation as if she had plunged her hand into cold water.

"Another person saw her go through the hedge, and he observed, that he could see the hedge through the figure as she glided into the field.

"It is whispered that this unfortunate lady was an ancestress of the original proprietor of the place, who married a man she adored, contrary to the advice of her friends; and too late she discovered that he had taken her only for her money, which was needed to repair his ruined fortunes; he, the while being deeply enamoured of her younger sister, whose portion was too small for his purpose.

"The sister came to live with the newly married couple; and suspecting nothing, the bride was some time wholly unable to account for her husband's mysterious conduct and total alienation. At length she awakened to the dreadful reality, but unable to overcome her passion, she continued to live under his roof, suffering all the tortures of jealousy and disappointed love. She shunned the world; and the world, who soon learnt the state of affairs, shunned her husband's society; so she dragged on her dreary existence with no companionship but that of two remarkable fine greyhounds, which her husband had given her before marriage. Riding or walking, she was always accompanied by these animals-they and their affection were all she could call her own on earth.

"She died young; not without some suspicions that her end was hastened-at least, passively, by neglect, if not by more active means.

"When she was gone, the husband and the sister married; but the tradition runs, that the union was anything but blest. It is said that on the wedding night, immediately after her attendant had left her, screams were heard proceeding from the bridal chamber; and that on going upstairs, the bride was found in hysterics, and the groom pale, and apparently horror-stricken. After a little while, they desired to be left alone, but in the morning it was evident that no heads had prest the pillows. They had past the night without going to bed, and the next day they left their home-she never to return. She is supposed to have gone out of her mind, and to have died abroad in that state, carefully tended by him to the last. After her decease, he returned once to the Bellfry, a prematurely aged, melancholy man; and after staying a few days, and destroying several letters and papers, to do which appeared the object of his visit, he went away, and was seen no more in that county."

Alas, for poor human nature! How we are cursed in the realisation of our own wishes! How we struggle and sin to attain what we are never to enjoy!

www.ingramcontent.com/pod-product-compliance
Ingram Content Group UK Ltd.
Pitfield, Milton Keynes, MK11 3LW, UK
UKHW021921190726
13853UKWH00002B/778